J

Finding
ESME

SUZANNE CROWLEY

GREENWILLOW BOOKS
An Imprint of HarperCollins*Publishers*

Author's Note

As a fifth-generation Texan, I've always been intrigued by old stories of the mythical, the magical, and the "real." In bringing Esme McCauley's world to life I was inspired by old 1800s ghost stories related in *The Best of Texas Folk and Folklore*, a publication of the Texas Folklore Society. This is particularly true of Harlan's ghost, who took him up and down Solace Hill at midnight. Ghosts demanding treasure are also a common theme of many Texas stories, as are "weeping" ghosts like the wailing woman of Bitter Creek. The match-blowing ghost in the henhouse was inspired by a late-1800s ghost tale related in *The Loblolly Book*, edited by Thad Sitton, as are the McCauleys' unusual bee-tending techniques. The story of Bee sleeping peacefully in her bassinet as a tornado passed over the house really happened to my grandmother and her mother, who suffered a head injury while desperately trying to reach her baby.

Finding Esme
Text copyright © 2018 by Suzanne Crowley

The text of this book is set in 12-point Sabon MT.
Book design by Paul Zakris

Library of Congress Cataloging-in-Publication Data
Names: Crowley, Suzanne Carlisle, author.
Title: Finding Esme / by Suzanne Crowley. Description: First edition. | New York, NY : Greenwillow Books, an imprint of HarperCollins Publishers, [2018] |Summary: "Twelve-year-old Esme and her best friend, Finch, discover dinosaur bones on her family's peach farm and are suddenly surrounded by people with nefarious motives"—Provided by publisher.
Identifiers: LCCN 2018022299 | ISBN 9780062352460 (hardback)
Subjects: | CYAC: Fossils—Fiction. | Dinosaurs—Fiction. | Friendship—Fiction. | Family problems—Fiction. | BISAC: JUVENILE FICTION / Family / Multigenerational. | JUVENILE FICTION / Girls & Women. | JUVENILE FICTION / Social Issues Adolescence. Classification: LCC PZ7. C88766 Fin 2018 | DDC [Fic]—dc23 LC record available at https://lccn.loc.gov/2018022299
18 19 20 21 22 PC/LSCH 10 9 8 7 6 5 4 3 2 1
First Edition

GREENWILLOW BOOKS

FOR ACREE CARLISLE, MY DADDY,
WHO TAUGHT ME THE POWER OF STORY
AND FOUND WONDER IN ALL THINGS

Peach Hollow Farm

CHAPTER 1

IF it hadn't been for my little brother Bo and me chasing fireflies, I would've never discovered the bones up on Solace Hill. It was my granddad Paps's tractor that first churned the bones up to the surface. My grandmother Bee says if not for their son (my no-good daddy) Harlan disappearing, Paps wouldn't have been on Solace Hill in the first place, digging for redemption. Bee was making peach pie in the kitchen when she noticed she could no longer hear the sweet hum of the tractor. She says our sorrows are linked together like our honeycombs, deep and cavernous, full of lonely hollows.

Paps's heart had simply stopped. Bee didn't have the gumption to move the tractor after he passed. That was three months ago. Now that tractor sat there like a giant rusty grasshopper. Sometimes I'd lie under it trying to feel his spirit—my gentle quiet Paps. Bee would yell from the kitchen door, "Esme McCauley, you know he's not there. GET OFF THAT HILL!"

Bee claimed Paps was in heaven, where God was tending to his hurts. But I don't know if I believed in heaven anymore, so every day after my chores, I'd lay under that tractor eyeballing the old grumpy horned toad who made his home there. I called him Bump. I'd like to think that somehow, some way, that's where Paps was, behind the ancient eyes of that horned toad. Paps's face was starting to slip away from me. I could hardly remember his voice, although it came to me every night in my dreams, like an echo, as though he were hollering from the bottom of a well, trying to tell me something. What, Paps? What is it? What am I supposed to know?

I'd never had much luck, even from the beginning. June Rain, my mama, had a terrible time with me in her tummy, could barely keep a bite down. Seems even back then she didn't want me. I came out eight weeks early, about as big as the big end of nothing, Bee says. Had to be kept in a warming incubator wrapped in a cotton cocoon over in Paradise. I was hardly bigger than a shoe. Then one night a few weeks after I was born, Bee snatched me back, said I needed the good warm beating hearts of kin. Every night she and Paps bundled me up tight and rocked me on their chests, my head as little as a butter bean, Paps told me.

I would never grow as big as all the other kids, the doctor said; only my feet and ears seemed to grow as the years went by. My face was pale white, my skin thin and translucent. One time Bee showed me my footprints and handprints on a sheet of paper from the hospital and it looked like a bug had crawled across it. I had giant eyes (Saucer Eyes), and a little mouth with hardly any lips (Butthole Mouth), and skinny legs (Skinny Sticks), and was just plain tiny (Thumby for Thumbelina). Bee said God would take care of it in the end. All my funny pieces would meld together perfectly and someday my special gift, my gift that was waiting for me, would work itself to the surface for all to see.

I stood at the screen door, my nose pressed against the mesh, praying, praying the rain would stop. I wouldn't be able to go up Solace Hill; Bee'd set up a howl if I laid in that mud under the tractor in the rain.

Bee was making peach pies again, just like the day Paps died, for the Holy Mercy Church of Abiding Faith's potluck dinner for the poor. Even though we're poor, there's always those that are worse off in Hollis, the town nearby, she says. I glanced back at her as she pressed her thumb along the edge of the pie making perfect half-moons in the dough. There were kettles on the stove bubbling with wonderful-smelling spices, and gingerbread in the oven.

And then . . . that's when, that's when it all began. A flicker of a shadow, a wisp of something outside. But I hadn't even turned my head from Bee. Had I? You know when someone is staring at you from behind and you just know it? Bee and I locked eyes for a moment, and she tilted her head, like Bump does sometimes, as though asking, *What? What, Esme?* Since Paps died, I'd felt those steely eyes of hers watching me as though I was a pot waiting to boil. I turned to the screen, but nothing was there, just the endless *tppp, tppp, tppp* of the rain as it splattered on the screen door.

June Rain? Had it been her? No, she'd been on the front porch a few minutes ago when I'd run in from collecting eggs. She'd been sitting in her rocker like she always does, cutting out photos of movie stars from magazines and putting them in the thick scrapbook she's had forever. Some days when she's up to it, she helps out at my Aunt Sweetmaw's Just Teasin' Beauty Parlor, but she doesn't leave our house much anymore. Since my daddy Harlan left for good, June Rain's been in a bad spell as long as a Texas drought. She hadn't even looked up at me when I'd walked past her with my shirt billowed out like a sail, cradling several dozen eggs.

Suddenly my toes started to tingle; you know that numbly feeling you get when you've sat cross-legged too long watching Saturday cartoons or listening to your teacher drone on and on during storytime? I didn't like it one bit.

I started lifting my feet up and down in sort of a march, to see if I could make it go away. Bee looked

5

over at me as she put another pie in the oven. "What in the good damnation are you doing?"

"I have a charley horse in my feet," I answered her. That's what it felt like, a little bit.

"In both of them?" She frowned, and then a soft look of worry crossed her face. "I don't want you going outside today," she said. "Especially not up there."

Despite my best efforts, my feet continued to hum and tingle. "Bridge Over Troubled Water" was playing on the radio from somewhere in the house, the gentle melody rising and falling with the tingles in my toes. Suddenly Old Jack, Paps's dog, jumped up on the other side of the screen door, then another jump, and another, whining to get a good whiff of all the smells—sweet peaches and sugared gingerbread and doughy flour and melted butter—and Bee clapped her hands at him. Had it been the shadow of Old Jack I'd seen a few moments before? The shadow that'd started my toes burning?

And then behind Old Jack, a flitting blur, a streak in the rain. I watched as it moved toward

Solace Hill, the bee-buzz in my feet rising up my legs before disappearing. I let Old Jack in, then pressed my nose against the screen. *"Shhhhh,"* I whispered down to him, petting his head. He licked at the screen, strangely trying to get right back out.

"Esme McCauley, you know he's not there," Bee said, her voice startling me. I turned to her. "You let go of that hill, honey," she said in a soft-as-cotton way, so unlike her. She put the peach pie in the oven and gave the oven a horse kick, for it was always on the fritz like most things around here. Then she braced her arms on the stove and stood still as a statue. I leaned forward, wondering what she was going to say.

"Why?" she whispered. "Why?"

Was she talking about my no-good daddy Harlan? I had an image of him, the day before he disappeared, sticking his whole hand in one of Bee's peach pies and just grabbing a big ole handful. Bee had swatted him away and told him to go fix the back-pasture fence, 'cause Miss Lilah's geese were getting in and eating all our peaches. And then he was gone. "It's for good this time," June Rain had said, somehow knowing it was more than a trip to Paradise for cigarettes.

Bee went back to work on the peaches. She never, ever smiles, and her name is fittin' 'cause she is cuddly as a hornet. I curled my toes up and down to make sure they were back to normal as I looked at Bee, hoping she couldn't see what I was doing. Bee is tall, taller than any other women in Hollis, and slim as one of her witching sticks. She wears her gray hair long, on the side, gathered at the end in a clip like a tiny fish tail. Sweetmaw was always begging Bee to come to the Just Teasin' so she could give her a modern hairdo, but Bee said she wouldn't let Sweetmaw Hennessy and her scissors near her if it was the last day on earth. There's bad blood between the two that's older than Egypt.

"Are there ghosts, Bee?" I asked her, closing my eyes, thinking of what I'd just seen out in the rain.

Her head shot up; her glasses slid down her nose. "What kind of question is that?"

I focused on a dusting of flour on her cheek. She always had something on her that was not supposed to be there, like peach fuzz, or a smudge of oil from fixing the Bee Wagon. One time she had a cicada shell riding around all day in her hair and she didn't even know it till my little brother Bo pulled it off and stepped on it, sending a loud crunching noise across the kitchen. Bee didn't have time to worry about such things, or to smile or frown, or to tell us she loved us. She was too busy taking care of the peaches, the bees, and all of us.

Just then June Rain drifted by the door, Bo trailing behind her like a shadow, plastic army men clutched in his hands. I don't think June Rain even knew he was there.

A while after Bee'd left to go deliver the food, and June Rain had gone to take her long daily nap, Bo disappeared, which was a good indication he was up to no good. Old Jack clawed at the screen door frantically. The rain had slowed down, not enough for me to go up to Solace Hill, but enough to go find Bo.

My brother Bo has always been wild as the hills, but as sweet as cherry plums. Bee says he's a bona fide ring-tailed tooter, always in mischief and always on the move, and that's just how little boys are. She's not worried about him; those sorts always grow up to be something 'cause they use all that energy in a good way and become go-getters and doctors and stuff. His teacher at preschool, though, after dealing with him just one day, called Bee and June Rain in and told them he has some scientific "full of crock" whatchamacallit problem. All I could decipher from the hushed conversation was the word "hyper."

Old Jack ran ahead of me like a rocket, zig-zagging through the peach trees in and out of the patches of rain-darkened sunlight. I chased him to the henhouse where we kept Bee's prized Buckeye hens. I'd already picked the day's eggs, but more than once I'd found Bo sitting in the hay and suck-ing the innards straight out of a pale brown egg. "Bo?" I called before going in. The hens inside were having a conniption fit. I leaned down in front of the small shack and poked my head in. It was strangely dark. "Bo?" I called again into the ruckus. Old Jack stayed behind me as he knew he'd be in big trouble if he ever went in the henhouse, but he was whin-ing and yelping like all get out. *"Shhhhh! Shhhhh!"*

I soothed the squawking hens. Dozens of feathers floated around in the dark like there'd been a pillow fight.

There was a tiny space with a tiny door next to the henhouse that was often one of Bo's hiding spots. I carefully opened the door and crawled in. My toes had started to buzz again. It was dark as night. "Bo?" I knew there was a box of matches that I wasn't supposed to touch on one of the ledges. I pulled a match out and struck the edge, and the small storage room lit up in the soft glow of the tiny flame. Suddenly there was a sound, like someone drawing in all their breath and letting it all out. Like when you blow out your birthday candles. *Whoosh!* The match blew out.

I quickly lit another one. *Whoosh!* Darkness. Someone, or something, had blown out the match again. I reached back to find the knob and shot out of there, barely feeling my feet because of the tingles.

And there was Bo, holding three prized Buckeye hen feathers, laughing. But I knew he hadn't been in that little room with me. Something else had.

"What's wrong, Esme?" he said. "You look like you saw a ghost."

I tried to smile and yelled, "I'm gonna catch you!"

He turned, laughing, and ran off toward Solace Hill.

A cold wind, the kind that tells you the rain is leaving, started to blow as Bo and I ran through the orchard, chasing fireflies. Bee said the fireflies were disappearing more and more every summer, and it made me sad.

At the base of Solace Hill, the buzzing started in my feet again. I ignored it as I peered at the gentle pinpricks of rain on the sweet clover. The clover grew in clumps up the hill, surrounded by butter-colored stumps of jutting stone. Bo ran ahead of me, laughing as he reached for the elusive fireflies, who would dance just out of his grasp. I ran after him, but Old Jack stayed behind, stiff as a sentinel, a low growl emitting every now and then from his throat.

It was just a moment later that I tripped over something hard, a rock that hadn't been there before 'cause I knew every inch of that hill like I knew the back of my hand, like I knew every foot of Peach Hollow Farm. Paps's tractor must have churned it up, and the rain must have unveiled it. I blinked, the wind knocked out of me from the fall and my nose throbbing from landing face-first on rocky earth. Something dripped on my hand. Blood. I'd given myself a bloody nose. I started to stand up just as I saw a shape. I stood back in awe.

It wasn't a rock. I leaned down and peered at it closer, holding my hand up to my bleeding nose. A bone. Not a stone or a rock. It was a bone! I stood up quickly, my heart dropping to my feet. Paps? Oh, God! Harlan? Could it be my daddy? I stood stock-still, shivers going up and down my spine, staring at that bone. Then I turned and chased Bo back down the hill after the fireflies. Like ghost embers in the dark they were.

Bo ran into the house, letting the screen door slam right in my face. He opened his hand and a fire-fly flew wildly around the kitchen. Bee was at the kitchen sink washing up the dishes. I slowly walked in after him.

"Where was the tooter this time?" she asked over her shoulder as she scrubbed a pie pan. Bo reached for one of the gingerbread squares, thick buttered pieces she'd saved for us on a crisp kitchen towel.

I froze: feeling the room spin as images of bones and blood swirled around my head. I couldn't even lift my hand to my nose to stop the bleeding. It dripped, dripped, dripped on the wooden floor. Old Jack, still on the other side of the screen door, whined and swished his tail.

"Esme's bleeding, Bee!" Bo yelled between mouthfuls of gingerbread.

Bee dropped a skillet in the sink with a loud clank. She walked over to me and lifted up my chin, squeezing my nose. "Get me a leaf from one of the peach trees, Bo," she said. Bo was swatting at the firefly he had trapped high on the screen. "Get it now, Bo!" Bee yelled. He ran out the screen door a minute later and ran in with one. She carefully folded it up into a rectangle. "Here," she said to me. "Open your mouth." I opened my mouth and she gently tucked it under my upper lip, then put her two fingers on top, with pressure.

"Stop shivering, honey," she told me. "It will stop in a minute."

But I couldn't. Not after what I'd seen.

"Now tell me, what happened out there?"

I knew she wasn't just asking me about the fall, about my nose. She knew there was more. I wanted to tell, I did, but I couldn't. I couldn't even if I wanted to. I closed my eyes, everything swirling around in my head. Bo let Old Jack in and he laid down at my feet and licked my toes.

"Stop shivering, honey, or the bleeding won't stop," Bee said.

"I can't, Bee, I can't." *Something's got ahold of me. Something's got ahold of me.* "Why he'd have to leave us, Bee?" I whispered, feeling like I was gonna faint. I was talking about both Paps and Harlan. Both of them had left me.

Bee, still holding her fingers gently on my lip, looked me in the eyes. "Paps was an old, old man, Esme. He had a full life."

I knew now this wasn't the whole truth and Bee knew it, too. My grandma's specialty is knowing things, knowing and finding things that no one else can. She was keeping half of it to herself, like she always did. I'd known my whole life that something was missing from Paps's story, all of our stories, like a great big puzzle piece. The one that made all of the other pieces make sense.

"There," she said, lifting her fingers. "All better."

But when I looked into her eyes, she looked away. I ran upstairs then, my heart beating fast. I jumped in my old rickety bed, threw the covers over my head, and tossed and turned it seemed forever before finally dozing off. I dreamed of white feathers raining down and bones churning up through the dirt, a tiny light in the darkness. *Whoosh!*

CHAPTER 2

I woke with a start. There was a slow, throbbing pain in my nose. Then I remembered. I'd found *bones*. I'd found bones up on Solace Hill. I lay in bed awhile, watching raindrops catch on the window, my white chenille bedspread tucked up under my chin. It was pouring again. I nibbled on the knots in the chenille, like I did when I was worried about something, those gnawed-down knots over half the bedspread representing my life. After Paps died, I'd stayed in the quicksand cocoon of my bed nibbling on those knots for a week, till Bee finally yanked me out. Bee says I carry too many worries in my heart and it's gonna explode if I don't learn to let them fly away.

I rolled over and pulled the bedspread over my

head. I couldn't do anything about those bones just yet. Not in the rain, and not with Bee's antennae up. I'd have to sneak back tonight. I clenched my eyes shut thinking about it all. Had I dreamed it? My numbly-tingly feet, the flash of shadows in the rain, the henhouse *whoosh!,* the fireflies leading us up and up and finally—that *bone*! My heart sank, wondering what it could be.

I still remember the day my daddy Harlan left for good. I'd watched from my bedroom window as he drove down the gravel drive in his white Chevy pickup, slowly, so slowly that for one ridiculous moment I thought perhaps he was thinking about turning around. I knew that *she*, my mother, was watching from somewhere in the house like me. A cloud of dust swirled behind his back wheels, and I could still make out the rainbow splatters on the tailgate where countless cans of paint had spilled. If I squinted, it almost looked like one of his paintings.

Harlan McCauley is an artist, but no one around here understands what he does. Bee describes his paintings as "ain't-no-picture" paintings (not to mention a waste of perfectly good paint). Amidst all of the swirls and blobs, most of his paintings have June Rain's beautiful face in there somewhere, haunting us at every angle. But since no one round here wants one of his "ain't-no-picture" paintings, he became a house painter. The ironic thing is, people in Hollis hardly can afford to have their house painted either, so he has to make his living by leaving, moving from town to town drumming up what little work he can.

But that day he left, three years ago, I knew it was for good. And so did June Rain. She threw all his paintings into the yard. Before Bee hauled them to the trash heap, I managed to save one with half of June Rain's face obscured behind giant turquoise and pink swirls. I put the painting behind my dresser, but it sticks out, the left eye calling Harlan home.

I know Bee tried to find Harlan. I saw an old newspaper from San Antonio one time in her sewing basket and there was an ad in there: "Missing: Harlan McCauley. Itinerant house painter. Tall, thin boned. Dark haired." And our phone number. That's all it said. My daddy, summed up in ten words. Despite it all, I still thought he'd come back, at least I did for a while, and I'd watch for the dust and his white pickup coming up the drive. Bo kept pestering me about it till finally I lied and told him Daddy was on a long trip and coming home soon.

Bee is a finder. She can find just about anything, but her specialty is water witching. She pulls a switch from one of our peach trees and bends it like a boomerang, and everything that's been tossed out to the world comes back to her. Somehow she just knows where to go and when she gets there, that witching stick points down to the earth, like magic. But nobody really needs her much to find water, not like in the olden days.

It's everything else they want. She found Vera Godly's Busbee's Abdominal Supporter for the Stout, otherwise known as a girdle, hanging on the flagpole in the Hollis town square, and Lottie Broadway's car that someone had joyridden around town, then left at Bitter Creek with a bunch of beer bottles rolling around on the floor, and Reverend Foley Hopper's runaway horse who was over courting another horse at Bent Creek Ranch. Lost keys, dogs, cats, cows, everything you can think of and more. She hadn't found Harlan yet, though.

Some call us peculiar, but Bee says her way of finding things is God-given. Just as God told Moses to use a rod to find water, God tells her where to go. But even if folks gossip about Bee McCauley, everyone always ends up at Peach Hollow Farm, one way or another, wanting something from her. Bee says I have her finding gift, but it's tucked down deep. It's something she's known since I came out early, quiet as a lamb, from June Rain's tummy. My eyes took in the room, looking for something. I just haven't found it yet. She said I would know when "the finding" found me. I would just know. And there'd be signs ahead, like an icy wind before a tornado. Is that what had happened yesterday?

I asked Bee once that if she could find someone's lost car keys, why couldn't she find my missing daddy. She said he'd gone so far away she can't see him anymore. Sometimes I go in the bathroom and pull out Harlan's Rise Aftershave Balm and squeeze a little on my hand and rub it on my nose. Then at least his smell is with me for a while. And Bo sleeps with one of Harlan's old paintbrushes under his pillow.

I could barely make out the outline of Solace Hill through the rain. My heart seemed to turn over. Then a flutter, a movement in my peripheral vision. But it was only Sugar Pie, our horse, chomping on one of the peach trees. Bee called her the Great Houdini 'cause that horse was always discovering a way to get out of her pasture, old as she was. She must've knocked down another line of the fence, and that meant Miss Lilah's geese might be coming for an unwanted visit, too.

I knew I'd better go get Sugar Pie and check the fence because peaches and honey brought in about the only money we had, except for the occasional dollar here and there people paid Bee for finding things. Most times they gave us goods, like a sack of grain or a coupon for a burger at the Sonic.

I knew that Bee worried mightily about us, even though she said God would always provide. But most times he didn't. Recently I'd found a letter from the

Hollis Grand National Bank torn up and thrown in the trash. There were words like *foreclosure* and *demand* and *money* and *August*. I figured it meant Bee had till August to come up with the money, or something bad was going to happen to us.

I pulled on a white T-shirt, my overalls, and the beaded moccasins Harlan had brought back from one of his trips. I stared at myself in my long mirror, wondering when I was going to fill out the training bra Bee had bought me in Paradise, like the other girls did last summer when we were all turning twelve. Perhaps this summer. Then again, maybe not. Nothing ever happened to me, at least not when it was supposed to. *But I'd found bones up on Solace Hill.* I closed my eyes a moment, taking a deep breath.

The rain had trickled down to a fine mist. At least I wouldn't be fighting Sugar Pie in the rain. I heard June Rain stir in her room next door, and I thought how it was June now and it was raining. Was she born on a day like this? Sweet and lazy? Whenever it rained I liked to think it was her birthday, for she'd never told us when it was.

Harlan met June Rain when she was sixteen at the Trinity Baptist Traveling Revival Show when they came and set up their big billowing white tent outside Hollis. Bee says those tents are full of fools and her son Harlan brought one home. No one knows where June Rain came from before that, and since she doesn't talk much I guess we're never going to know. She guards her secrets well, but she's no match for Bee.

I'd gathered up few precious clues about her in the years: two bubblegum-colored dots on her ankle, a snake bite, she told me, that she'd barely survived; a pale blue movie ticket stub stamped "Majestic" with the words "meet me" written in faded pencil; and a heart-shaped locket inlayed with mother-of-pearl. With her wide, dark eyes; flawless, cotton-puff skin; and long, dark-as-night hair, she had the look of a princess or one of those movies stars she was crazy about. She definitely didn't look like anyone else around here, that's for sure. The boys in town thought she looked like Cher and sang "Gypsys, Tramps and Thieves" at her back when she walked downtown to the Just Teasin'. Sweetmaw would come out and whap them on their rears with her broom and tell 'em to get on home.

Of course I didn't look anything like Cher. No sirree. Bee says I look more like Harlan but I didn't know what that meant anymore because I hardly remembered him. June Rain says he's handsome and that she was caught in his web like a helpless bug. I often wondered if it was the other way around, though. I looked in her eyes sometimes and thought they were the most beautiful things I've ever seen, like dark inky oceans, with mysterious things swimming beneath.

The only thing I remember distinctly about Harlan was his brown work boots, which looked like his "ain't-no-picture" paintings with all those splatters of paint. One day Bo painted rainbows across the tip of each boot and said that they were now Daddy's rainbow boots. Even though I was mad at Harlan for leaving, I knew I'd give anything to see those boots coming back through the screen door and June Rain running into his arms. She always forgave him no matter what, and sometimes I don't think I can forgive her for that. But now, I'd do anything to see her smile again.

Someone was pounding on the back door. The tight curl of hope in my heart unfurled just a tiny bit. I heard someone thundering up the stairs, and my door burst open. Then Old Jack bounded in, Bo behind him.

"Sugar Pie's out again and Finch Aberdeen's at the door. Says Miss Lilah's gone," Bo told me.

CHAPTER 3

My first memory of Finch Aberdeen: we were five and he was sitting behind me at church, yanking on my hair. When I turned around and stuck my tongue out at him, he told me I was uglier than a fence-post buzzard and I told him he was a Mr. Potato Head like all the Aberdeens were, 'cause I'd heard Bee say it once, although really, Finch didn't look anything like the rest of them lowdown Aberdeens. I made him cry. Then Bee pinched me for causing a scene even though I was just repeating something she said. Better to keep your mouth shut, she says, and seem a fool than to open it and remove all doubt. She should talk, though; her mouth gets her in trouble more than there's summer fleas on a backyard hound.

Finch has been my best friend ever since, even though Bee says I'm too old to be roughhousing and playing make-believe with a boy. Bee thinks it's not fitting anymore, and it's high time I started wearing dresses instead of my old overalls and moccasins. She even bought me some Odo-Ro-No deodorant from the Ben Franklin, said my armpits were stinking to high heaven. But I'd hidden it under the sink in the bathroom I shared with Bo and June Rain. I wasn't ready to grow up. It'd had been a long time since I'd played with my Chatty Cathy doll, but I wasn't ready for Maybelline Kissing Potion either. Besides, my bra looked the same in the front as it did on the back. I was never gonna grow up, whether I wanted to or not.

Finch was trying to grow his hair long like his brother Granger and the other Hollis High boys, who were all trying to look like David Cassidy, but it wasn't quite working out because of his cowlick. The cowlick was sticking up funny now as he stood at the door, his freckles tinged blue-green from the cold rain. Finch had a habit of rubbing his nose, pushing his thick glasses up, and then smoothing his cowlick down in one fell swoop, but it just made him look like Prince Valiant from the comic strip, with glasses.

"What's wrong, Finch?" I asked him, biting into a peach. I glanced nervously at Solace Hill. My stomach lurched as the image of that bone sticking out in the rain flitted through my mind. Over Finch's shoulder I could see Bee coaxing Sugar Pie back to her pasture, Miss Lilah's geese waddling in a line behind them. I knew Bee knew I'd seen Sugar Pie and had taken my sweet time. She shooed the geese to get a move on. Miss Lilah's geese had long been a sore spot for Bee. Sometimes in the winter, Bee would bring a folding chair out to the pasture, turn them over one at a time, and pluck all their best feathers, then she'd send them back to Miss Lilah looking bald as the day they were born. But we'd all have nice fresh pillows.

"Miss Lilah's gone," said Finch, sucking on candy, his words slurpily garbled. The smell of root beer wafted through the screen. Ah, my favorite. Bottle Caps. I opened the door and reached out my hand and he begrudgingly pulled the packet of Bottle

Caps out of his back pocket and tilted it till one came out and rolled around in my palm. I curled my fingers, meaning more please, and he shook out a few more. If one of us was lucky enough to procure any candy, we shared it with the other; it was a sacred pact. I gobbled up a Bottle Cap. Since Paps had been gone, I hadn't had any money for candy. He used to slip me a dime now and then when Bee wasn't looking.

Bee says Finch is empty-headed, that he wakes up and it's a new world every day. But Finch Aberdeen is the smartest person I knew, the smartest boy in all of Hollis Junior High. He just didn't show it in the normal way. Maybe he couldn't hit a home run or make a touchdown, but he could tell you about every skyscraper in Dallas, and that the site for the Parthenon in Greece had to be cleared of dinosaur bones before it was built, and the Leaning Tower of Pisa is banana shaped and leans over twelve feet, even though neither of us has every traveled farther than Paradise, which is fifteen miles away from Hollis.

"Miss Opal went to give Miss Lilah breakfast

this morning and found her bed hadn't even been slept in," Finch told me.

Miss Lilah Ames is ancient, old as the hills. She doesn't get out much anymore, so about a year ago Bee made Finch and me start visiting her once a week. We bring her and Miss Opal Honeycutt some of our peaches and honey and whatever else is blooming in Bee's garden.

Opal Honeycutt lives in an old, rickety cabin behind Lilah's house. At one time Miss Lilah's family had been rich. Opal was the daughter of the Ameses' housemaid, but they were raised together as sisters. She was old, maybe even older than Miss Lilah. She says she doesn't know when she was born.

"Maybe Sweetmaw picked her up for her appointment at the Just Teasin'," I said.

Bee was coming up the front walk now, wiping hay off her plaid shirt. That's her uniform, dull mud-colored work shirts, the kind rancher men wear, and old khaki dungarees rolled up haphazardly, one leg usually higher than the other. Her hair billowed out around her like she was some old wind-blown witch.

"Who's missing?" Bee asked. She already knew it was a person, not someone's teeth, or car keys, or milk cow. She frowned at Finch.

"Miss Lilah," Finch answered, pushing his glasses up. We followed Bee inside to the kitchen.

"Old woman like that," Bee said with a sniff, for even though she made us visit Miss Lilah, she never liked her for some reason. "She likely wandered off." Bee looked out the window as she washed her hands. I recognized that faraway I'm-thinking-leave-me-alone look. She got that look before she knew something, knew something sure as salt.

"I know Miss Bee," Finch answered. "But that's what Miss Opal's worried about. Yesterday all Miss Lilah could talk about was her baptism in Bitter Creek when she was ten and how she was sure she was going to drown right there where she found the Lord. And 'cause the creek rose during the night from the rain, Miss Opal's beside herself, sure she's in the water."

A shiver ran through me. There's a legend about Bitter Creek that says that sometimes amidst the rolling water, you could hear the ghost of a drowning woman calling for her lost love.

"Only fools are sure, Finch. You know Miss Opal's not quite right." But neither was Miss Lilah. Finch and I had seen her slowly decline in the last year, the light leaving her. Bee closed her eyes a moment. "No," she said firmly. "She's not by water. But we better go. Hold on, let me fetch my hat." Bee never went to find something without her hat. "Esme, you go fetch me a willow branch. A good one. The rain will make it better for bending."

Then we three got in the Bee Wagon. Several years ago Bee bought a 1952 Pontiac ambulance from Paradise that doubled as the Paradise hearse. Life is about leavings and comings, Bee reminded us when we'd stood around it, not believing what she'd brought home. Bee had Harlan paint the twenty-year-old car a cheery blue, and Paps had tuned up the engine. It even had the white eyelet curtains still in the back. But sometimes you just can't perfume a hog.

Bee revved the wagon and put her in reverse even though Finch was still getting in and hadn't closed the door yet. Miss Lilah's geese were in the back peeking out through the curtains. We waved at June Rain and Bo, who were watching us from the front porch. June Rain had those hare eyes that worry me sometimes, all soft and lost. Old Jack barked and ran after us till we turned down the gravel drive that led us away from Peach Hollow Farm.

I was mesmerized by Bee's large, sun-spotted hands clutching the black leather wheel of the Wagon. I closed my eyes a moment, remembering when those old hands helped the firemen carry Paps in from Solace Hill. He was so stiff, they had to pry his fingers open. In one fist was a faded photo of Bee when she was young. I didn't even recognize her, she was so beautiful, so elegant. There was something in his other hand, too. But when they pried it open, I only got a hauntingly slow flash of a small golden coin before Bee snatched it. I've never seen it again.

Miss Lilah Ames still lived in the house she was born in. Her property butted up to the Aberdeen place. Finch told me in the car that the last few days he'd seen Miss Lilah take the long walk to her mailbox and back at least ten times a day.

"Maybe she's waiting for a letter," I said. I knew about waiting for letters. June Rain made that same walk to our mailbox every day, but nothing ever came, not even a postcard to give us a clue where Harlan had gone. No sirree, not a word. Ever.

"No," Finch said. "She's forgotten she walked out there by the time she steps back on the front porch. Then she goes out again."

Miss Opal had hobbled over to the Aberdeen house that morning when she couldn't find Miss Lilah, raising the alarm. No one even thought of calling the police. Not when Bee McCauley lived round yonder down the road.

Bee pulled the Bee Wagon into the driveway. Miss Opal met us at the house, leaning on her cane, the same cane she'd been leaning on forever.

"Something different this time, Miss Bee," she said. "Something different. I'm mighty worried. All this looking back at the past. She's all stirred up about something and—"

"That's all right, Miss Opal," Bee said. "I'll find her." She said it with conviction, as if she'd said the sun was going to come up. She walked past Miss

Opal with her witching rod in front of her. It was already bent, jiggling at the end, like a hound dog that's picked up a scent.

"Maybe it's best if you stay here, Miss Opal," Finch said to her. "It'll be all right."

Bee was already fifty feet in front of us. Miss Opal stood there, both hands on her cane, tears forming in her eyes. Finch went after Bee. I knew well enough to stay back some. Give Bee her air. She didn't like anyone right next her, said it crowded her "signals." But of course, Finch had forgotten.

He soon came running back to me, nursing a pinched arm. We then followed a ways behind Bee, the only sound our shoes squashing in the mud. Last night's rain was now just a fine mist in the air. I never realized how far back the Ames property went. We scampered up and over several ridges, Bee marching like a soldier, her hat squashed down low. Suddenly she stopped. I signaled to Finch that it was all right for us to catch up with her now.

When we reached her, her witching stick was pointing up, hovering gently. We looked to where it pointed, and there was old Miss Lilah, sitting on the low-slung limb of an oak tree. It was the strangest thing I think I'd ever seen. Her eyes were fixed on something in the distance. We approached and Bee tended to her, talking to her softly. But I followed Miss Lilah's gaze. Across the valley was Peach Hollow Farm, and looking like the steeple of an ancient church, there was Paps's tractor up on Solace Hill. Shivers went up my arms then, and my toes started that low hum, tiny and warm.

"Miss Lilah," Bee said softly, "time to come down." Miss Lilah was soaked from head to toe and shivering like a plucked chicken. She must've been out all night in the rain, sitting on that limb.

"He was on that hill, shouldn't have been, dad-gummit," Miss Lilah said. She'd never uttered any cuss words in our presence, but then again she'd hardly said a word during our short visits, only nodded sweetly as we drank iced tea with mint on her front porch.

Bee had a funny look, her lips pursed tightly like she'd swallowed vinegar. I waited for her to ask Miss Lilah what she meant, but Bee kept her mouth firmly closed.

"Who?" I asked. My toes were throbbing. "Who was on the hill?" But I knew. I'd seen Paps up on Solace Hill about a week before he died, standing there a good long while, puffing on his cigar, looking out at our farm. I'd watched him from my window and something down deep told me not to follow him that day, not like I usually did.

"My Homer," Miss Lilah said. "He's on the hill. I see him on the hill. It's because of her. Shouldn't have married that hussy."

She meant Bee! I almost laughed. Bee was twenty years younger than Paps. I'd never heard how they met, only that Paps kept to himself on the farm and rarely came to church and everyone round here had assumed he'd never marry.

"Come on, Miss Lilah," said Bee. "We need to get you home before you catch your death. Miss Opal can make some hot tea."

But Miss Lilah wouldn't let Bee take her arm. "You know very well, Bee, about that . . . that hill, those ghost lights going up and down, up and down, up and down. . . ."

Bee put two fingers gently on Miss Lilah's lips.

Their eyes met and then Miss Lilah looked away. Bee was usually so brave, but at that moment she turned to me with a look so fearful it sent shivers down my spine and all the way down to my toes which, by the way, were thumping now.

Finch and I helped Miss Lilah climb out of the tree, and just as I was handing her off to Bee, Miss Lilah gripped my hand and said, "He was looking for something on that hill, honey. Find it and he'll be at rest."

We rode home in silence except for the sound of Finch chewing Bottle Caps in the backseat. After we dropped him off and Bee parked the Wagon in the drive, I asked softly, "Why was he digging, Bee? What were the lights Miss Lilah was talking about going up and down Solace Hill?"

"Fireflies," she said flatly. She gripped the steering wheel a moment, staring straight out the windshield at our farm, breathing deeply. I looked over at her, willing her to look at me. But she pulled the keys out of the ignition and went inside.

I had to wait until after dinner and it got dark

before going back up Solace Hill. June Rain was listening to the radio in her room and Bee was washing dishes. Bo was playing with his army soldiers on the floor. I hummed along to "Raindrops Keep Fallin' on My Head" as I stood at my window, watching the sun as it slipped down behind the hills like a gold coin. My heart was racing and my toes were still tingling with the "knowing" that I'd found something big up there. Something life changing. What had Miss Lilah said about Paps? About him being on Solace Hill? Bee had said he wasn't here anymore, that he was in heaven, but I didn't think so. He was still there on that hill, trying to tell me something.

I tiptoed past June Rain's room. I ran through the living room and grabbed one of the crazy quilts Bee's always making when something's on her mind, and I ran out the front door with it.

The rain had turned up huge clots of mud on Solace Hill. The ruts leading up the hill through the sweet clover to Paps's tractor were still there, his roadway to nowhere. Why had he suddenly gone up there with the tractor? I'd asked Bee and she'd said he was turning up a new pasture for Sugar Pie to graze on. Anyone with an ounce of sense could see the hill was too steep for our old horse.

My moccasins, already wet and dirty from tromping through Miss Lilah's land, were now even more caked with mud. I felt as though I was walking in quicksand.

When I made it to the top, I was too scared to search for the bone right away. A bird flew in the distance as the sun slipped beyond the horizon. I stood there taking deep breaths, looking down at our old farmhouse, which sorely needed new shutters and a good coat of paint, and beyond it at our acres of peach trees and open pasture. Several miles away were the faint twinkling lights of Hollis. I carefully crawled under the tractor and spread the crazy quilt out. I hummed a church hymn that Bee sang sometimes at the top of her lungs when she hung the washing out on the line. "Old Mountain. Old Mountain. Lead me up the Old Mountain. I see Thee a coming O'Lord, I see Thee a coming . . ."

I caught movement out of the corner of my eye and I jumped, hitting my head on the tractor. But it was just Bump, perched on something emerging from the mud to the right of the tractor. Very slowly, ever so slowly, my eyes followed the length of Bump's ridgey back. He was sitting on the bone. And he wasn't but three feet from me. I could be lying on top of a skeleton, for goodness sake.

I scrambled out, then Bump scurried down the hill. Breathing hard, I quickly brushed the mud off my pants.

I took a breath and squatted down next to the bone. Gently, ever so gently, I put my fingers on top of it. After a few more deep breaths, I brushed away some of the dirt. More white, strangely opaque, feathered with fine cracks. Whatever was buried here had been here a good long time. *A good long time.* I leaned down and put my face right up close, my nose almost touching it, my heart racing. I realized how alone I was. With that bone. I stood up and raced down the hill.

As I made my way back to the house, I spotted June Rain wandering through the peach trees, her eyes wetly brown in the darkness. When I tried to coax her inside, she lifted her finger up to her lips,

"*Shhhhh.*" She clutched my arm, then cupped my cheek with her other hand. "*Shhhhh.*" Her fingers smelled strongly of cigarettes—Harlan's old Salems, the ones she'd always hidden from him. I twisted from her grasp, turned, and ran to the house.

CHAPTER 4

"**Look** over yonder, who do you see? God's gonna trouble the water. Who's that yonder dressed in white? God's gonna trouble the water." All morning while we'd been singing hymns at the Holy Mercy Church of Abiding Faith, I'd been thinking about ghosts and whether they were real or not. About the ghost of the drowning woman in Bitter Creek, and why she'd hadn't gone on home to heaven. I sat mesmerized by the waggling spittle on Reverend Foley Hopper's chin as he droned on and on. Bo was next to me scribbling on the collection envelope with a big fat crayon. Every few minutes when he opened his mouth to chatter in his non-church voice, Bee would pop in a lemon drop.

Someone once stole the collection platter from

Holy Mercy. Bee found it out back with her witching stick. There were just a few pennies still inside along with a black beetle who'd made his home there. She had a notion who did it but decided not to say anything. Bee told me whoever stole it must have needed money desperately to justify the theft. She left one of her witching sticks straight across the pulpit like a cross until Reverend Hopper brought it back to Peach Hollow saying it's best to sweep in front of your own door; some things people already know in their hearts, and they don't need to be shown it.

What had God been trying to show me? What had Paps been trying to show me? Or the ghost in the henhouse? Was it a ghost? What had been flitting about in the rain? And what about that bone? All morning I'd been shaking, my knee popping up and down till finally Bee reached over and pinched my thigh. I was so scared I tingled. Something was happening in my life and I didn't know what it was.

Paps was gone, Harlan was gone, my mother may as well be gone, and there was hardly anything left. I'd never felt so alone in my life. I daydreamed about hopping on a bus and just seeing where it took me, escaping from Peach Hollow Farm. But Bo looked up at me just then and grinned his big ole tooter grin and I knew I'd never be hopping on some bus and disappearing. I would stay here and put what was left back together.

Sweetmaw sat on the other side of the church as far away from Bee as she could, or maybe it was the other way round. For three generations the Hennesseys always sat together in the front row, and their mama Louella would be sore hearted to know they were so spread apart now. Their older-than-Egypt bad blood went further back than when Bee supposedly stole the famous Hennessey bees, which Sweetmaw says were rightly hers by inheritance. June Rain told me once that secrets run deep on Peach Hollow Farm.

The Hennesseys, at one time, had made honey at Honeycomb Farm on the south side of Hollis as way back as anyone could remember. Louella Hennessey thought naming her two daughters Bee and Sweet was fitting. But Bee swears that Sweetmaw is not as sweet as everyone has come to believe. More like a fig that tastes like a lemon as soon as you bite into it. But I'd always wished she were my grandma instead of bossy ol' Bee. Sweetmaw Hennessey is so sweet and kind, always smiling with a nice thing to say about everyone.

Vera Godly, the town's official spreader of bad news, sat in front of us waving a fan back and forth. I glanced behind me and saw Dovie Cade in the back with Rose Galloway and Mady Whitshaw, the most popular girls in my class. They wore matching telephone-wire rings twisted into big flowers, supposedly all the rage with the Paradise girls. Dovie's mama worked at the cosmetics counter at the Ben Franklin, and they were always hanging out there painting their faces with the sample lipsticks and testing out all the stinky perfumes. The Ben Franklin had been me and Dovie's special place once.

I caught Dovie's eye. We'd been friends forever long ago. Now she hardly looked at me. I realized then that Dovie was not really pretty at all, she just seemed pretty 'cause she basked in Rose's sunshine, and underneath all that makeup was the plain girl who used to follow me around on the playground. About a month after Paps died, a bunch of girls had cornered me in the bathroom to ask me how I was doing. Dovie had quietly slipped into one of the stalls. Rose had patted me on the back saying how sorry she was. Later Finch had yanked something off my back. A single square of paper covered with the names kids had called me my whole life and a few new ones. It hurt even now, thinking about it. Dovie might not have written it, but she'd done worse; she'd hid in the stall and let it happen.

Bee was watching me funny as I wiggled around and shivered, giving me that don't-fidget-in-church look. She'd made me wear a white cotton dress with fat little cherries on it and funny underwear with lace on the edge and shiny white Mary Janes that looked like shoes a five-year-old would wear, especially since my feet were so big. Bee got them from Lottie Broadway in exchange for Bee finding Lottie's car. The dress showed my white knobby knees and the underwear itched my rear end to high heaven, and the shoes, well, they just looked stupid.

I turned the pages of the hymnal and sang loudly.

Us McCauleys weren't known for our singing abilities. Bee once volunteered for the choir and was told there was no room, although there were only six of them up there including Treva Stump, whose voice sounds like a yowling cat. Bo crawled around underneath the pew to tie Vera Godly's shoelaces together. Bee yanked him back, sat him upright, and popped another lemon drop in his mouth.

Finch Aberdeen sat behind me with his mama and his brother Granger, who was sleeping with his head back, his mouth open so wide surely God could see his Adam's apple from heaven. Finch's daddy Spoon was absent as usual; he was probably sleeping off last night's whiskey. Bee's had to find him many a time. Once he was passed out in a chair at Sweetmaw's and somebody had put sponge curlers in his hair and painted his nails pink. Bee says we all got it bad, but the Aberdeens got it worse with their no-good daddy and Finch's no-good brother who can't find the right wagon to load. Sometimes Bee puts baskets of peaches and squash and beans by their back door. Finch told me his mama brings them inside before his Daddy sees 'cause he don't like charity.

Finch was kicking the pew and making funny faces at me when I looked back at him. He lifted his Mr. Potato Head ears up and down, his special trick, trying to make me catch the church giggles, those giggles you can't stop once you start. I ignored him; I had enough on my mind.

After church I looked for Sweetmaw, but she was talking to Sheriff Truett Finney (that old fat fellow, big as Dallas, Bee says) by his patrol car. The sheriff didn't like Bee and how she poked her nose in his business. He had even threatened to throw her in jail once.

Bee turned on her heel and announced she needed some things in the Ben Franklin. I grabbed Bo's hand and headed toward the Bee Wagon. No way was I going to the Ben Franklin. Dovie Cade would be there with Rose and Mady, where they'd be getting free grilled sandwiches and Frito pies and thick chocolate malts. All 'cause Dovie's mother Dee Dee worked there. My heart turned: Dovie hadn't even come to Paps's funeral, and I don't think

I could ever forgive her that, whatever her reason.

"Esme," Bee called. "Come along." Bo ran glee-
fully ahead and I begrudgingly followed, Finch
behind me. There'd be no Sunday dinner at his
house. He always came home with us after church.

Bo ran immediately to the candy case and pressed
his nose up against it, making one long streak as he
moved down the length of it looking at the butternut
chocolate crumbles, the orange slices, the licorice,
the root beer barrel candy, and the Tootsie Rolls.
Bee marched to the back of the store and I avoided
the soda fountain where all those horrible girls
with their matching flower rings sat on the stools
already slurping down their malts. I walked past all
the things that used to bring me such happiness—
the Dawn dolls, the paper doll books, Bazooka
Joe hard-as-rock bubblegum that came with a car-
toon, the rhinestone rings that Dovie's mom used
to let us play with, the velvety change purses, and
quarter-cent tin toys. Finch took Bo over to the toy
section, which was like putting a hungry shark in
a goldfish bowl. I ended up in the tool aisle looking for some tools to help me unearth the bone but

knowing I didn't have the money to buy anything. Suddenly Dovie's face appeared on the other side of the aisle between cans of hornet spray and fishing bobbers.

"Why does everyone hate me?" I asked. One of those tiny ten-cent balls painted like the earth came bouncing over from the toy aisle. I caught it and squeezed it.

"No one hates you, Esme," she said. "They don't even know what happened. Not really. Not all of it. They just think you're different. They think you're weird."

I had no idea what she was talking about. Yes, us McCauleys were peculiar. A long line of us, going back to Louella Hennessey who could predict the weather better than the *Farmer's Almanac*, and Louella's mother May who could foresee the future in her coffee grinds. But why did that matter? She never used to care. There was an awkward pause and I turned to walk away.

"Are you all right?" she asked quietly.

"You never even came to his funeral," I said, turning back to her.

She lowered her head. "I was too upset, and scared," she said.

Scared. "Are you kidding me?"

She wouldn't meet my eyes. Bo hopped by behind her, a pirate's hat on his head, two big teddy bears tucked under his arms like torpedoes. Finch was nowhere to be seen, but two aisles over, a cloud of bubbles floated up and over the ladies' underthings and men's hankies aisle. They floated over us gently, then moved on.

"You don't remember the play set?" Dovie asked. "Recess?"

No, I had no idea what she was talking about, I could hardly remember anything about last spring. But a sickening feeling started rising up in me.

And then an image of Dovie and me swinging on those old metal swings. It had been a clear day, no bad weather in sight. The other girls were trying on lip gloss and pawing through their purses. The bell rang; the kids trickled back into school. Dovie continued to swing, high, higher.

"You screamed at me to get off the swing," Dovie said. "I was mad, mad at you for yelling at me like that. But I got off, and right then it happened. Lightning struck the swing set, Esme. I saw the electricity snake along the whole thing like a ribbon of fire, and you just kept on swinging. I came over and coaxed you off, and it was like nothing had happened, only your hair was standing on end, straight up above you pointing at the blue sky. I helped you inside. And then you told the teacher you had to go home. You were mumbling about a storm. No one had seen the lightning, though, only me."

I raised my eyebrows. I didn't remember any of this.

"And from what I can gather," she continued, "you made it home and saw Miss Bee running up the hill."

"To Paps," I said, realizing it now. "And I didn't get there in time." Then vague memories of later that night, Bee scrubbing my hair in the bathtub, me sobbing, asking "What happened? What happened?"

Rose Galloway called Dovie's name and Dovie's face disappeared from view. I closed my eyes, feeling sick to my stomach. A few minutes later, Bee herded us past the cosmetics counter and out the door. Dovie's mother Dee Dee waved at us, and my toes buzzed. I had a clear vision of her grandmother's prized wedding ring, lost for years, underneath the face cream counter, covered by a piece of petrified bubblegum. I crouched down and yanked it out. I set it down on the counter in front of Dee Dee's astonished face and followed Bee out of the Ben Franklin.

Bee tore down the road back toward Peach Hollow Farm. Bo sat in the front seat, letting a paper whirligig spin out the window. He'd slipped it past Bee and she didn't even seem to realize he had it.

I whispered to Finch, "The day Paps died, did I have funny-looking hair?"

He puckered up his lips. "Yep, as I recall you came in from recess looking like you'd stuck your finger in a light socket."

He said it as though I'd asked him if the sky was blue.

"Why are we whispering?" he asked.

I caught Bee's eyes in the rearview mirror—those

searching eyes, waiting for something, looking for something. I turned away and watched the passing fields of sassafras and sprawling live oak whiz by.

When we pulled up to the house, I didn't look at Solace Hill. But I could feel it pulling me, tugging at me, like a cool swimming hole on a blazing hot day. Finch stepped on the back of my shoe, leaving an ugly black smudge. He laughed, and I pushed him away. I didn't want to see him anymore today; I didn't want to see anyone. I wanted to be by myself up on that hill.

"What's got you all in a fluster?" he asked, grinning. His cowlick had managed to pop up. It looked like a flag on his head. For the briefest of second I wanted to tell him everything, but I couldn't. I didn't even know what was happening.

"Nothing," I mumbled. My eyes betrayed me and I looked at Solace Hill. Something passed through me then, achingly, as I imagined Paps up there going in circles on the tractor. And I'd been sitting on that swing minutes earlier when lightning hit. I felt Bee's presence behind me then in the driveway;

she'd paused, and the shivers went up my back. The moment seemed to go on forever, us sharing something, that knowing, that vibrating, that something-needed-to-be-found feeling.

But it was my secret for now, *mine*, whatever was up there, whatever was happening in me. *It was mine*. I was going to have to be very careful; Bee could sniff out a secret a hundred miles away and I had about as much chance as a rooster egg that she wouldn't find out what I was up to. She nudged me forward up the steps.

June Rain was in the kitchen. She'd set the table and was making something doughy and cinnamony—something that needs ingredients, and mixing and baking—and putting it in the oven. I suddenly had a memory of her cooking chili for Harlan. It tasted like it had been cooked in an old stinky barrel, but Harlan seemed pleased that June Rain had made the effort. And here she was actually baking. There was even bacon frying in a pan, and scrambled eggs with vegetables chopped up in them, like how you get them at the Dinner Bell Café. I couldn't believe it. I got a little sick feeling in my tummy, though, wondering what she was up to, knowing somehow that any change involving June Rain had consequences. Bee and I exchanged a look. She was just as surprised as I was. Even Old Jack froze, his head tilted curiously at her.

Finch helped himself to a pinch of the dough that June Rain had left on the counter before Bee scooted us out of the kitchen.

"You go on, you two, start picking some of the early-ripe peaches. I'll call you in for lunch when it's ready."

I went upstairs and changed out of my dress and stupid shoes and back into my overalls. I left on the new underwear with the lace. I think I actually liked it a little bit, although I'd never admit it to Bee.

I walked as slow as I could to the orchard, Finch ahead of me whistling, Bo running behind us. Old Jack zigzagged through the trees after a jackrabbit. Nothing I hated more than picking peaches. I've been picking peaches for over a hundred years, at least it seems like it. Bee says it is our life-blood, and someday I'll enjoy it. But not today. Not ever.

After we'd been picking awhile, Finch said. "You

sure are quiet today, Esme." He reached in his pocket and pulled out a pack of Candy Cigarettes gum and held it up proudly. He must have purchased it at the Ben Franklin and Bo's whirligig, too. Candy Cigarettes were one of our all-time favorites, but neither of us had money usually. I took a purple-tipped one and put it in my mouth.

A bee was droning around my head, so I moved under another tree. I feared bees more than any-thing in the world, even more than spiders, which was very strange since we had beehives out in the woods (the famous bees that Bee supposedly stole from her sister) and gathered our own honey. Bee thought I was just being difficult. But I'd always been afraid of them, those bees, even from before I could remember.

I wanted to be farther away from Finch, too. He knew me too well. He knew most of my secrets and I could tell him anything. Bee said that Finch Aberdeen had no arrows in his quiver and she'd been making him as welcome as a wet shoe lately, but I still liked him, wet shoe, empty quiver or not. He'd never turn on me. But I wasn't going to tell him about the bone like I wasn't going to tell him about my new lace underwear or that I was hoping I'd fill out my bra soon. I wasn't going to tell anyone.

"Is it because of what Miss Lilah said yesterday about Paps?" he asked a few moments later, one of the candy cigarettes dangling out of his mouth.

"No," I said as I bit into a peach and sat down under the tree. "Why would you say that? We all know Lilah Ames's got a hole in her screen door and is not playing with a full sack of marbles anymore. Poor Miss Opal."

"My daddy says Miss Lilah was fancy on your paps once upon a time." Finch pulled the cigarette into his mouth and started chomping on it, then blew a giant pink bubble.

"I think we can all guess that," I said, thinking about her sitting on that low tree limb in the rain like she was sixteen, her moon-pie eyes on Solace Hill.

"But your paps didn't marry her because Bee Hennessey put some spell on him. That's what my daddy says. Says all of your line is mighty strange and peculiar and maybe . . . "

I threw my peach at him and it left a wet mark on his church shirt. "Why would you say something like that, Finch Aberdeen? And who'd believe anything that comes out of your daddy's mouth anyway?" I knew that would hurt. But no one was gonna call my family crazy.

Finch pushed his glasses up his nose, and looked at me. We could say almost anything to one another, tease each other to no end, but our families were off-limits. He'd started it, though, talking about my paps and Bee. He walked away, back toward the house. *Ow!* My arm started to tingle like it was on fire. That bee had stung me. My eyes welling up with tears, I calmly pulled the stinger out as a large, angry welt appeared.

Bee was in the kitchen making a lemon curd. She'd sent Finch home after June Rain's fancy scrambled egg lunch since we'd hardly looked at each other all through the meal. The bittersweet smell of lemons wafted up to my room and I could hear the rhythmic *click click click* as she sliced them on the cutting board. *Click. Click. Click.* Something was on her mind. June Rain and Bo were watching Gumby and Pokey in the living room; the goofy, cheerful up-and-down lilt of the TV voices sounded so strange in our house. *Click. Click. Click.*

I went downstairs and froze in the kitchen doorway, shock running through me. Sweetmaw was at the screen door, still wearing her pillbox hat and lavender polyester church dress, her purse clutched at her side. She held one of her famous Hennessey pies—cherry I could tell from the dark pink peeking through the crisscrossed crust. Bee had stopped chopping her lemons, her knife frozen in midair.

"June Rain invited me for dessert," Sweetmaw said, through the screen. "She called me." Bee looked at June Rain, who'd suddenly appeared and was washing dishes. Her face was obscured by her dark silky hair, but somehow I knew there was a slight smile there. The whole scene unsettled me, because June Rain did not bake, did not smile. She usually just let the world spin around her. I always feared the world would someday stop and she would just get off. I ran to open the screen door for Sweetmaw and she walked into Bee's kitchen as though she came every Sunday for dessert.

"How's the Just Teasin'?" Bee asked as she continued to chop the lemons. *Click. Click. Click.*

"Busy like always," Sweetmaw said.

Bee rolled her eyes 'cause she knew that wasn't the truth. Most everyone in town was poor and business was slow.

"Hoping June Rain might come back soon," Sweetmaw said. "She always worked magic on the older ladies."

Sweetmaw put the pie on the table and Bee shot a look at it. There was something there—a memory perhaps, but the kind that feels sweet at first and is then followed by something bitter and sad. I watched them and wondered how they could be sisters. Sweetmaw was as short as she was wide and wore her hair in one of those sprayed helmet do's that was popular a long time ago. And unlike Bee, who I'd never seen wear as much as even a hint of lipstick, Sweetmaw's face was always perfectly done up, her eyelashes like furry caterpillars, her chubby cheeks pinked with blush.

June Rain put out dessert plates and forks and

Bo came running in just as the pie was cut into pieces and we were all sitting down. Bee wouldn't take one bite of hers and just peered at Sweetmaw. The rest of us ate our slices and asked for more. Bee and Sweetmaw didn't say one more word to each other. Not one word.

Later, when Sweetmaw was leaving, she lingered on the steps, looking back into the house. I was on the way to my room but stopped in the hall to listen.

"I've heard it was one of our pies that won him over Bee," Sweetmaw said to Bee through the screen.

"You've forgotten I was a Hennessey. The recipe was mine, too," said Bee, sounding like a teenage girl.

"But not the bees," Sweetmaw said.

"They don't belong to anyone, Sweetmaw. They're bees. They followed me the day I married Homer, followed us as we walked from the church."

"Everything just happens, Bee. It just happens, right?" Sweetmaw sounded sad now, so unlike her.

"I didn't steal him," said Bee as the screen door slapped shut. And then I heard a soft good-bye, Bee's voice cracking. A minute later when I peeked into the kitchen, Bee still lingered at the door, her face pressed into the screen, her hand up in a wave. Then she turned and threw the remains of the pie in the trash.

My daddy Harlan loved the bees. They were restless, just like him. He made them new hives every year with two-by-fours. He'd nail his paintings of large colorful flowers on the sides. He put the hives in the woods, seeming to know where the bees wanted to be. When he moved the hives to a new spot, he called them with a cowbell, and like a big black cloud they followed him to their new home.

Even though I was afraid of the bees, Bee insisted I come with her to the hives the next afternoon. She'd been taking care of them since Harlan left.

"Why do I have to go?" I said, following behind her, sulking. She didn't say a word, just walked stiffly on, and I stuck my tongue out at her back. A flock of ravens flew over us. I thought about that bee swarm following Bee and Paps as they left the church. What else had she taken with her when she'd married him? The way Sweetmaw acted, it was as though Bee had taken the whole world with her.

"It's time," Bee said after a little while. "We need the money."

We need the money. Each summer we usually collected four or five gallons of honey. Bee drove all over the county selling Bee's Honey and it was well prized in the kind of shops that sold soap with leaves and sticks floating in it, and incense, and cute porcelain pigs. Bee was carrying a small bucket with a butcher knife and a fork. I carried a long stick with wads of cotton, scraps from her quilting heap, wrapped in a ball on the end. When we finally reached the hives, I stood a ways back, rubbing my sore arm, which Bee had fixed up with a soft bandage and salve.

"You ain't ever gonna conquer your fears unless you face them head-on," Bee said over her shoulder as she worked at prying the lid off the first hive with a hammer. When I didn't move, she tilted her head in that cut-it-out gesture she gives to me and Bo sometimes. So I stepped forward, keeping my eyes averted from what she was doing, which was basically opening up Pandora's Box. I focused on one of Harlan's purple flowers. A hyacinth. I blinked and leaned in closer. He'd painted a tiny image of June Rain's face peeking out from a petal as though she were a fairy tale princess.

"Did you really steal Sweetmaw's bees?" I asked, looking away from the painting and down at my feet.

"They were leaving anyway, just like me," Bee responded. "Those bees just followed, that's all." She lit a match, and I lifted the stick so she could light the ball of cotton.

"Then why have you and Sweetmaw been so mad at each other if it wasn't about the bees?"

She waved the flame around the hive like a great enchantress. The smoke made the bees retreat deep into the recesses of the honeycomb. Bee reached into the hive with the fork and pulled a huge ball of honey out, letting it drip into the bucket. Then she carefully nailed the lid back on the hive and we moved on to the next one. She never answered my question, but I knew she wouldn't. I thought about what she'd said about the McCauleys' sorrows,

linked together one after another like our honeycombs, and wondered if we'd ever be happy.

After the trip to the hives, Bee kept me busy with
more chores. It was like she knew, *she knew,* as she
always knew things, that I wanted to escape.

Old Jack wandered into my room after dinner
and nudged me. Paps had found him on the bank
of Bitter Creek, looking like he'd been spit up from
the river. Once Paps nursed him back to health, he
didn't look old; he just had those eyes that said, *I'm
old; I've seen everything.* So Paps named him Old
Jack.

Old Jack nudged me again, then put his paws up
on the windowsill, looking out toward Solace Hill.
"Okay, Old Jack. We'll go. We'll go," I said.

Tiptoeing past Bee's room, I stopped when I
saw the door was ajar. I listened a moment, then
slowly opened it and stood there taking in all her
smells—cotton puffs, some awful stringent bath
soap, and the faint tinge of dust and forgotten
things. Her room was sparsely furnished—an old
twin bed hardly better than a cot, a side table, and

bureau—old junky pieces that looked like they'd lived most of their life disintegrating in an attic. The only nice thing she had was the rocking chair Paps had rocked me in as a baby, back when I'd been snatched from Paradise. Back when I was just a translucent butter bean.

I walked straight over to the bureau. Old Jack waited for me at the door, whining. Something told me to open the left drawer. Maybe that gold coin was in there, that delicate gold coin Paps had had in his hand when he'd died. I opened the drawer and fumbled around in the ancient buttons and reached underneath an old scrap of quilt and touched a small folded-up piece of paper. It was a telegram from Harlan asking for bail money from some town in Louisiana. It was dated a month ago. I tucked it back in the drawer when I heard Bee stir down in the kitchen and I ran out of the room wondering if she'd helped him or let his butt rot.

The night my baby brother Bo was born, the sky was a strange violet-tinged blue. Although he showed up late, smelling of beer and tobacco, Harlan was there, and when he got a look at his new son, his perfect son, so unlike me, I thought this time, this time, he's gonna stay. And I think June Rain thought so, too, for she was smiling so sweetly, like I'd never seen before. But Harlan left a week later, sure as salt, and June Ran hadn't smiled like that again.

And just then, just as I was thinking about Harlan and Bo and June Rain, I found it. At the base of one of the trees, right where I'd seen June Rain, there were three small cigarette butts. I picked one up and held it to my nose. Old Salems. Harlan's brand. I dropped it like it had burned me. Someone had stood here under the trees, long enough to smoke these, watching the lit windows of our house. Old Jack sniffed at the butts, then barked. A cold wave washed over me as I turned and ran on toward the hill.

Old Jack and I trudged up Solace Hill as the light from the setting sun slanted down in wondrous purple rays. I'd brought along a small shovel and pick I'd found in the storm cellar, and a lantern. A chorus of crickets sang, and I could hear Sugar Pie snorting from her pasture. Miss Lilah's geese squawked behind the newly fixed fence, their heads straining through the wire to chew on our grass.

I got down on my knees and started looking for the bone and panicked that it had all been a dream, a nightmare, or perhaps only a wish. But then a burst of sunlight illuminated the slope, silently, swiftly, and my feet tingled when I saw the beautiful glimmer of white in the dirt. Old Jack bounded up to it and wagged his tail.

I pulled out the shovel.

CHAPTER 5

Bump the toad joined us, and I could swear he was eyeing me. Old Jack whined, his tail wagging slowly back and forth. My toes hummed, vibrated. I knew whatever was down there was going to change my life forever. I took a deep breath and dug softly, reverently, filled with dread that I was unearthing a holy grave. The dirt, softened by the rain, gave beneath my shovel and I threw one large clump over my shoulder. I dug faster and faster. My heart began to race as I cleared away the soil and more and more dusty white came into view. I stood back a moment to catch my breath.

It was huge, whatever it was. *Huge.*

Enormous. Relief poured through me. It wasn't the bones of a *person*, but something else. I took another deep breath and stared at it. I knew uncovering it was going to take a very, very long time with my little shovel and pick. Maybe months, even. But something told me I'd found something spectacular on Solace Hill. And something had lead me to it. The ghost, the spectral, the fireflies? Paps? I continued to dig, more slowly now, more reverently. I didn't want to hurt or damage it, whatever it was.

Hours later, just when Bee started calling for me to come in for bed, another clump of dirt fell away and I could see the outline of one long, *very long*, angled tooth. Surprised, I quickly tried to stand but fell back on my rear instead. My heart began to thump wildly. I heard the crickets sing and Sugar Pie neigh. I blinked. I blinked again. Old Jack, who'd been sleeping soundly a few feet away, opened one eye. I leaned forward, studying the tooth. Bee hollered again. It was big, this tooth. At least three inches long—a long triangle with a sharp point on the end. It was like the shark teeth some of the boys at school wore around their necks on leather cords, but lots bigger.

"What the heck?" I gasped. Old Jack backed

away, whining, then barking, till I called him to come over and look. "It's all right, old boy," I said. "It's all right." He sniffed at the tooth. I set down my tools and covered what I had dug up best I could with Bee's crazy quilt. As we ran home through the orchard, a fine mist illuminated the peaches like sugared candies. Once we got close to the house, I could see June Rain's silhouette up in her window, face pressed against the screen.

Bee was waiting for me in the kitchen doorway, smoking a cigar, its lit tip like a firefly hovering in the dark. It was one of Paps's, and it smelled like mowed hay after rain. I felt my stomach drop watching that ember, thinking about what I'd found earlier, those cigarette butts, and what it might mean, and how Bee knew things, but didn't really know, not really. Thinking about the matches out in the henhouse, the fireflies leading us up the hill. All of it.

We locked eyes a moment and a small shiver went up my back. I waited for her to say something. But she turned away and I brushed past her, shivering, and ran up to my room.

Sometime in the night, Bo crawled into bed

with me, snuggling up under my arm. He hummed sweetly off-key, harmonizing with the rhythm of the rainfall. I dreamed that night of a big-toothed monster, of Finch's blue-green freckles, and June Rain's peach-tree eyes. *"Shhhhh,"* she whispered to me. "Don't tell."

The next morning I woke up thinking about what I'd found on Solace Hill and if I should leave well enough alone. I'd once asked Bee what she'd ever do if she found something really bad, and she said she couldn't choose what God led her to and I wouldn't either when my time came. *When my time came.* All my life Bee had told me I'd get her gift, but I wasn't sure I wanted it now.

When I went down to breakfast, I paused at the top of the stairs. June Rain's door was open. I knew her soft footsteps, her slow movements, her silence, her stillness; wherever she was in the house, I was aware of her. But I couldn't hear her, so I tiptoed into her room. Everything was always trim and tidy—her bed made, clothes neatly folded, almost as though she didn't live here. When I was little

I always looked under the bed, checking for her suitcase, worried she was gonna leave and follow Harlan. I walked to the window where I'd seen her last night and peered out. She was in the yard hanging clothes on the line. Bo was laughing and running through the sheets.

She'd taken Harlan's portrait of her from my room and leaned it on top of her dresser, her sad face staring back at me amidst all the swirls and blobs. I picked it up and something fell on the floor.

It was a postcard. On one side was a big cactus in the desert with "Arizona" drawn fat and cartoon-like across the top. I slowly turned it over. It was addressed to June Rain McCauley, Peach Hollow Farm, and was dated two weeks ago. There was no writing, just a crooked heart painted in blue. I held it to my nose, smelling his Rise Aftershave Balm and the faint, stale odor of smoke. *Harlan.* I started to put the portrait back and saw there were more postcards propped up against the wall. They were from all over the country. None of them had a note, just smiley faces, hearts, and other scribbles, tiny versions of his ain't-no-picture paintings. Harlan never really did know his letters. Bee said he couldn't spell his way out of a watering can. But all this time I'd thought we'd hadn't heard from him and he'd been sending these messages to June Rain. *And she didn't tell me. Didn't tell any of us.*

I quickly looked under her bed, my heart exploding with worry, and pulled out her suitcase. I slowly, slowly opened it as though it were a coffin, like I'd done so many times before. But it was empty.

The kitchen door slapped, startling me, and as I hurriedly put the cards back behind the portrait, the edge of a black-and-white photo caught my eye. The picture was of Harlan, leaning against an old-timey gas pump at a filling station. There was a prairie beyond the gas station, with a majestic blue mountain looming in the background. His heavy-lidded eyes were smiling back at the camera. I wondered who'd taken the photo. Was he traveling with someone? He was happy, wherever he was. But different than I remembered him. I quickly stuck the photo in the bottom drawer of my bureau, where I kept the photo of Bee, the other Bee, the one we didn't know, the beautiful one, who'd walked on her wedding day with a swarm of bees over her head.

After picking peaches for Bee all morning, I rode my bike down our rutted road over to Finch's house. Finch's house looked like someone had punched it. The front porch sagged, a couple of windows had cardboard taped across, and a sad row of blue Christmas lights, missing every third light or so, rimmed the roof. There was a rusted-out pickup truck in the front yard and clothes out on the line that had been there so long, they were polka-dotted with mud and grime.

Finch's mama answered the door in her house-coat, her hair rolled up in orange juice cans and a dark shadow under one eye. I could hear the Aberdeens' mangy dogs barking from somewhere in the hollows of the house.

"Finch here?" I asked, after she eyeballed me up and down. Visitors weren't welcome at the Aberdeen house. I was practically the only one who had the courage to venture up their front porch. Spoon Aberdeen's temper was legendary. He spent more time in the county jail over in Paradise than out of it.

"Got anything from your grandma?" Pearl Mae asked, looking down at the small basket I was carrying.

"I got peaches," I said, handing it to her.

She snatched it from me and said, "Hold on, honey." The door slammed shut and then a few minutes later Finch appeared with a set of purple Clackers. He was counting as the balls flew up like little gymnasts, then came back down. They'd been the rage at school in the spring, but neither of us had money to buy them.

One of the Aberdeen dogs shot past Finch like a rocket and then straight down the road. Finch didn't even blink, just kept on clacking and counting.

"What do you want?" he asked. "Fifty-five, fifty-six." *Clack. Clack.*

The secret about what I'd found up on Solace Hill rose to my lips like a sweet bubble. But I couldn't share it. I knew I couldn't. Not yet.

"I wanted to know if you'd come with me over to Miss Lilah's," I said. "I want to ask her more about what she said."

"Sixty-two, sixty-three." *Clack. Clack.* He frowned. "About what?"

"You know, about what she said. About a light going up and down the hill."

"Sixty-eight, sixty-nine." He hit the Clackers so hard I thought my ears would bust.

"Will you put those stupid things down?" I hollered.

He begrudgingly stopped. He leaned in toward me and sniffed. "You smell funny."

I blinked. "I'm trying out some new perfume Bee gave me. Blushing Rose."

"Well, it stinks to high heaven."

I left my bike at Finch's house and we walked over to Miss Lilah's. The afternoon sun, like an orange Creamsicle, sat low in the sky, and there was a soft breeze carrying the smell of freshly cut grass. Miss Opal was out in the garden picking beans when we walked up. She looked over at us as we approached, wiping her forehead with a rag she pulled from a pocket in her cotton dress.

"Is Miss Lilah here?" I asked.

"She is," she said. "We weren't expecting you. I don't have iced tea, or—"

"That's all right, Miss Opal," Finch said quickly. "It never tastes quite right anyway." I elbowed him hard, even though it was true. I think Miss Opal, getting on in her years like Miss Lilah, forgot to wash off the mint leaves, and I'd more than once seen one of the Aberdeen dogs peeing in their garden.

Miss Opal frowned. "Miss Lilah have her good days and bad days. Today's not one of the good ones." There was something there in her voice, a soft worry. "Something has stirred her up mighty fine the other day and she's been chewing on it since. My mama used to say we look back on our lives when we're afraid of what's in front of us."

"I promise just a few minutes," I said.

She nodded toward the house where Miss Lilah was rocking in a rocking chair on the front porch, and I could almost swear she hadn't been there when we'd walked up the drive.

"I thought you'd come back," she said when we walked up the steps.

Miss Lilah smelled like lavender and Johnson's Baby Powder and unaired, dusty attics. Her hair was freshly done in a neat helmet hairdo that was Sweetmaw's specialty. Miss Opal took her to the Just Teasin' every Monday, and June Rain used to do her hair sometimes, back when she worked a regular shift.

"You want to know more about what I seen," Miss Lilah said, her rocker creaking to a stop.

A shiver ran up my legs. "Go on," I urged.

Finch was leaning over the porch railing picking a flower and examining it; he knew every species of anything around here.

"Sometimes I can't sleep," she said. "That's all. Sometimes I wander at night. Can't help it. Not as though I was watching for him."

"Watching for who?" I asked.

"Homer," she answered. "Although I swear, I wasn't watching for him. After Harlan was born, anyway, I knew no hope anymore. But somehow I'd end up in the night on that tree limb watching Solace

Hill. And every night I'd see a ghost go up that hill, then go down that hill. The fireflies following both ways."

"A ghost?" I said. "Probably it was just the fireflies, Miss Lilah."

She turned and watched Miss Opal out in the garden. "I told her it was too hot. 'Too hot today, Opal,' I said, but she says the beans not gonna wait."

Miss Opal peered at us, shielding her eyes from the sun, the worry shining in them like soft beacons.

The porch began to tilt a little and I shut my eyes. Ever since Paps had died, Bee had been telling me to stay off that hill. Been watching me ever so carefully. *Sometimes you find what you don't want to find.* Maybe it had nothing to do with Paps. Maybe it was something that had happened before. But a ghost?

"We'll come back soon Miss Lilah, if you'd like that," I vaguely heard Finch saying. I didn't know when he'd popped up from the railing. I took a big breath and Finch grabbed my arm. He was looking at me strangely like I'd just sprouted two heads.

Miss Lilah peered at me. "Maybe best you stay off that hill, honey."

* * *

"Why was she talking nonsense about ghosts, Esme?" Finch asked me on the way back.

"Like you said, Finch, it's just nonsense," I answered.

Something tenderly rolled across my heart. It all had something to do with why Paps was riding his tractor that day up on Solace Hill, the last place a tractor should be. He was up there looking for something. Been up there the week before when I'd seen him, and Lilah, too.

CHAPTER 6

I was riding my bike back home from Finch's when Bee pulled up next to me in the Wagon and came to a creaky stop, the dust blowing in a powdery puff in my face. I put my bike in the back and got in. "Where you been?" she snapped. My stomach fell. I'd been hoping I'd find a way to sneak back up Solace Hill without her seeing me. June Rain and Bo were in the backseat, quiet as doves.

"Over to see Miss Lilah," I said. I glanced at June Rain, but her eyes were far away. I was very mad at her for not telling us about the postcards. But being mad at June Rain was like being mad at the wind, or the sky. Bo leaned over the seat and I gasped. The old crazy quilt, the one I'd used to cover the bone on Solace Hill, was wrapped around his shoulders. He peeked out of it like a pig in a blanket.

Bee hit the gas and we lurched forward. "She wasn't expecting you, was she?" She glanced over at me, narrowing her eyes behind her spectacles. She was wearing her finding clothes and had a freshly picked witching stick sitting on the seat between us. It had one lone, unripe peach on it. I knew exactly what tree she'd gotten it from because I knew every peach tree by heart. Bee varied her witching sticks depending on the weather and her mood. A peach witching stick meant she wasn't sure what we were gonna get.

"Humph," she muttered when I didn't answer right away.

Bee knew I was hiding something. She always said when I lied my nostrils flared, which let the devil in, so I turned my head and looked out the window so she couldn't see my nose.

"Where we going?" I asked, glancing back at Bo, wondering why he had the quilt and what he'd seen.

"Treva Stump called and said she has something for me. Wouldn't say on the line 'cause everyone was listening up and down the road." We have a party line on our road, which means everyone knows one another's business. "I could hear that Granger Aberdeen breathing heavy and Pearl Mae telling him to get off the phone, she had chores for him to do."

"Why they coming?" I asked, tilting my head toward the backseat.

"June Rain says she feels up to working at Sweetmaw's and we need the money bad," she said.

I nodded.

Bee continued. "Sweetmaw says lots of the ladies are getting their hair done for some tea tomorrow. Everyone want perms and no one does them better than June Rain. Right, June Rain?"

I knew June Rain wouldn't answer. Bee always talked to June Rain that way, like she's a baby or a dog that might miraculously answer back.

But she did, to my surprise. "I'm hoping to use a new technique. Sweetmaw says she has the Permalaster kits all the way from Chicago."

Those were practically the most words I'd heard out of her in years. Something sad passed through me, though, hearing her soft voice. I'd overheard Bee on the phone once talking to Doc Delaney when June Rain was having one of her real bad spells, when she wouldn't get out of bed for days, about some hospital up in Abilene. I heard Bee say no, the McCauleys take care of their own. We didn't have the money anyway. After she hung up she gave June Rain a dose of her Black Draught, made of fermented peaches and castor oil (and a secret ingredient), which she used on all of us in any situation. But it didn't work on June Rain. Nothing worked on her.

I stuck my head out the window, trying to get some fresh air as Bo exclaimed, "I get a kazoo from the Ben Franklin!"

"That's only if you're a good boy at Treva's, tooter," Bee said as she swerved the Wagon around a roadrunner. Bo slid into June Rain, laughing, and I thought perhaps I saw a tiny smile on her face.

I thought of the photo of Harlan hidden in my drawer. *All those scribbly postcards and you didn't tell us, June Rain.* Maybe she had perked up because she'd gotten one recently. *And those Salem butts in the peach orchard* . . . And he was nearby in Louisiana, not but a month ago. In jail, but still. I didn't want to hope, knowing how hope was usually dashed into a thousand pieces.

"Hey, Bee, do you think we can go to the library after Miss Treva's?" I figured I could find some books about bones with pointy shark-like teeth.

"What do you want at the library?" Bee asked, looking at me, eyes narrowed.

"I thought I'd get some summer reading."

She pursed her lips in that I-know-and-you-know-you-are-not-telling-the-truth way but didn't say anything. I'd never been a huge reader, "below grade-level reading comprehension," my report cards said. Bee tore them up every year.

Bee drove the Wagon up Main Street to the town square. We didn't have much in Hollis, not like Paradise. When their chamber of commerce erected a welcome sign that read, "Escape to Paradise," Hollis erected a sign that said "Come Home to Hollis." We didn't even have a Whataburger or a Tasty Freeze. Just the Ben Franklin, and the Dinner

Bell Café, and the hardware store, and the Sonic Burger. And, of course, Just Teasin' on the corner across from the Get-n-Go grocery store, which is half the size of the Get-n-Go grocery in Paradise.

June Rain got out and went inside, the Charisma perfume Harlan gave her for Christmas one year wafting behind her. I had to pinch my nose; it was so strangely exotic. She was wearing her best dress, the embroidered one with roses that Harlan had gotten for her in Mexico. She'd even had mascara on, and her eyelids flashed sparkly blue like she was going to a dance club, or planning on running into Robert Redford on Main Street.

Several men whistled at her and Bee leaned her head out the window of the Wagon and cursed up a storm at them. Although she's washed my mouth out with soap more than once, Bee knows more bad words than Spoon Aberdeen and got kicked out of the Circle of the Women's Missionary Quilting Club for using all of them in one sentence.

Bee backed the Wagon up, and Bo scooted to the middle of the seat, now wearing the quilt on his head. I kept my eyes straight ahead, not daring to look back again as we headed out to Miss Treva's on the south side of Hollis.

Miss Treva was waiting for us on her front porch, her hands on her hips. Whatever she needed Bee for, it was urgent, more urgent, I suspected, than the time Miss Treva's daddy lost his false teeth and Bee found them stuck in the trunk of a pecan tree. Seems he'd reached over and taken a bite of the bark and left his teeth there, but couldn't remember why.

Bee pulled the Wagon up in front of the house and told Bo to go play on a tire swing hanging from an old oak. He left the quilt in the car and ran off. He torpedoed himself through the middle of the tire and swung around on his tummy, laughing.

"Well, Miss Treva," Bee said, witching stick at her side, "what can I help you with? I hope it's something more exciting than your daddy's teeth."

Miss Treva's eyes were flitting around and she was hugging herself, hands clasped across her front, holding her elbows, although it wasn't cold out.

"What's Esme doing here?" she asked nervously.

"She's learning my witching." That was the first I'd ever heard of *that*. That I was here to learn something. "Whatever it is, it stays with us," Bee continued. "I know a little bit about everyone here, Miss Treva, and I won't ever tell any of it." It was everyone else who did the talking.

"Well, okay," Miss Treva said.

"So what are you missing?"

"My husband," Miss Treva answered.

"Your husband? Luther?" Bee asked in surprise. "I saw him yesterday after church sitting outside the filling station with Johnny Wa—" Bee stopped herself, but I knew where she was going. She must have seen Miss Treva's husband with Johnny Wallet. That's not his real name, of course. He got his nickname from picking wallets.

"He's up to no good," Miss Treva said. "A wife knows these things." There were tears in her eyes now. "He disappears every day, says he going in to the mill, but I ran into his boss yesterday and he asked me—'Where's Luther been? He hasn't been at the mill.' But Luther still got money; I found a whole big roll of dollar bills in his back pocket. And sometimes he gets up in the middle of the night, but I don't see the car lights goin' down the drive."

"He's not gone far," Bee said, looking around the property, narrowing her eyes. "I can tell you that."

"You mean he's right under my own nose?" Miss Treva sputtered, the tears running down her cheeks now.

Bee started walking around the house, but she wasn't holding her witching stick up yet. Miss Treva and I trailed behind her, watching her as she poked about—lifting up a trash can lid, a log on the log pile, and then opening the barn door. She fished down in some hay and pulled out a shiny silver dollar. She handed it to Miss Treva. Those are the best finds, she always says, those you're not looking for. The image of the gold coin in Paps's hand flitted through my mind. Then, without saying a word, Bee walked out of the barn, turned toward the woods that bordered the Stump property, and marched on like a soldier, her witching stick buoyed up by something unseen.

Miss Treva and I watched her go, then exchanged glances and went after her, trying our best to catch up.

"We'll be right back!" I called to Bo, who was

still happily spinning around on the tire swing, his fingers trailing in the dirt.

We followed Bee through the trees. She seemed to know what the stick was telling her, suddenly turning to the left or the right, like a hog in the brush being chased by a hunter. At one point a jackrabbit jumped out at us, scaring Miss Treva and me, but it didn't faze Bee. She was on to something for sure, but when my arms started prickling and toes vibrating, I began to feel that maybe we shouldn't be here.

"Bee!" I called after her, but on she went, because when she's on to something she doesn't stop till she finds it, no matter what. I could smell something now—like baking bread mixed with smoke and grit and something nauseatingly sour. Suddenly Bee stopped. We'd come to a deep clearing where the sun was trying its best to break through the trees in long slanting shafts. Bee was standing in one, illuminated brightly, her witching stick vibrating, and I could feel it, too, that vibrating, down deep in my bones. Slowly, ever so slowly, the tip of Bee's witching stick started turning down to the earth.

"What in tarnation!" Miss Treva gasped.

In front of us was the strangest contraption I'd ever seen—a hodgepodge of barrels and tubes snaking around a large vat with smoke coughing up out of a rusty pipe. Underneath it all were the embers of a small fire. Three scruffy-looking figures were sitting on a log. One of them, Luther Stump, stood up, pointing a shotgun at Bee. The other two just sat there with their mouths hanging open. It was Granger Aberdeen and Johnny Wallet. They were both holding tin cups.

"See, I told you Treva was up to something," Granger growled.

"Get outta here, Bee McCauley," Luther said, spitting in the dirt. "'Fore I shoot your meddling behind."

"You ain't gonna shoot anyone," Bee said, but I could hear the tiniest catch in her voice, a slight quiver that told me she was scared, too. She'd never found anything like this, no, not this big. "You boys know very well what you're doing is illegal. Sheriff Finney won't be able to ignore something like this. And Granger, I'm ashamed of you. Your mama has enough on her plate."

Granger, his eyes red rimmed and half open, looked down shamefaced.

I felt like I was going to throw up. I looked away, thinking how different Finch was from his family, from all of them. My heart was about to thump out of my chest. But I was also sad, sad for the Granger I used to know, the Granger who would give Finch and me noogies and sneak us M&M's during church, even if he called me Stinky Weasie and Finch Monkey Kettles.

Miss Treva stood behind Bee. "I thought it was that floozy from Paradise," she said softly.

"How'd you know about *her*?" Luther asked stupidly, brandishing his shotgun, and Miss Treva let out a sob.

"And you got more, don't you?" Bee asked Luther. "Where you hiding your other stills? In the water, I believe."

"You stay away from Bitter Creek," Luther snarled, shaking his shotgun.

It was quiet a moment and I thought of Bo back at the tire swing, happily drawing his circles in the dirt. I suddenly had an image of the swing empty,

Bo standing at the edge of the woods. No! I tugged at Bee's arm.

"Maybe we can come to some agreement," said Luther.

"Nope, I don't shake hands with the devil," said Bee, turning to leave. Luther stepped forward, lifting his shotgun again.

Bee grabbed Miss Treva's arm and we all started to walk away. Suddenly there was a shotgun blast, and we froze. Bee walked on, pulling us along with her. I peeked back and saw Luther with his shotgun still pointing up in the air.

Bee didn't say a word the whole way back into town, but I could see her chest heaving. Bo was in the backseat asking one question after the other. Bee told him to hush, her voice shaking slightly, and I couldn't believe it. My Grandma Bee was not all powerful. I turned and peered out the window. We picked up June Rain at the Just Teasin', then roared out of town, the white eyelet curtains in the back of the Wagon swaying to and fro. None of us said a word. June Rain stared out the window, a small postcard-smile on her lips.

"You gonna tell, Bee?" I whispered hoarsely a few minutes later. Thank God Bo hadn't seen anything. Thank God we hadn't been hurt.

Bee didn't answer me, just stepped on the gas, causing rocks to splay up behind us.

We rode the rest of the way home in silence.

That night for supper we had leftover sweet-pork beans with rice and jalapeño cornbread. Bee's hand shook as she stirred the pot on the stove, round and round, round and round. In all her years of witching I don't think a shotgun had ever been fired, least not that I knew of. She was usually rewarded with gratefulness, sometimes regret and disappointment. One time a century-old dead cat in a chimney. An old family recipe. A forgotten security box in Paradise. A rhinoceros horn brought back from a safari. Lots of things, but nothing like this. I washed up the dishes afterward, and Bee didn't even ask why I volunteered. Usually I disappeared faster than a raindrop in the desert.

She was sitting at her sewing machine in the front

room, stitching a new crazy quilt, when I snuck out, the *tap, tap* of her foot going up and down on the pedal reverberating in my ears. I ran through the peach orchard, swinging the lantern, throwing warm arcs of light across the trees. I'd hidden the pick and shovel back in the storm cellar in the field behind the house. That's where Paps used to come sometimes to hide from Bee and take a few puffs on the cigar he stashed up on a high shelf. The stub was still there, like the footprint of someone long gone. As I was swinging open one of the doors, I felt someone behind me in the semidarkness. *Harlan?* I swung around fast.

It was Bo, standing there with the crazy quilt around his shoulders, Old Jack by his side. "Bo, you too old for that," I yelled at him, snatching the quilt. Then I felt bad.

"I want to go with you," Bo said, staring at the June bugs as they buzzed around my lantern.

"Where'd you get this?" I asked, clutching the quilt to my chest. It smelled of summer grass and cider, melted cherry Popsicles, and Johnson's Baby Shampoo.

"Up there on Paps's tractor." He pointed.

My heart sank. "You see anything up there, Bo?" I asked carefully. Telling Bo a secret was the same as blasting it out to the whole world.

"Just a horn toad. It scared me, so I ran back down the hill."

I took a deep breath. Bump had been guarding my bones, of course he had.

"You go on home," I told him, lifting his chin so he knew I was serious. "I got some Wax Lips and Gold Nugget Bubble Gum under my bed; you can have 'em." I swallowed hard. It was a sacrifice, but I had no choice.

Bo turned his head a little, looking like Old Jack does when he's trying to figure something out, like if you are up to no good. But whatever Bo was thinking passed quick enough at the thought of candy. He turned and ran for home, a big smile on his face.

Old Jack followed me as I went up the hill. When I got to the top, I sat down to take in the wonder of it all. A soft breeze tickled my nose. Were there really such things as spirits? I thought perhaps Paps was here, maybe.

I held the lantern up close to that one ferocious, giant tooth. It was scary, but I knew it was gonna change the no-good, honeycombed bad luck we'd had all these years. I decided to name whatever this creature was for my great-grandmother Louella. Somehow they were connected, the long line of peculiar relatives in my family and that big bone. It was my Louella Goodbones, 'cause something good was going to happen. I just knew it. God couldn't send so many sorrows in a row without sending something good eventually. I wrapped Bee's crazy quilt tightly around me, then crawled under Paps's tractor with Old Jack. I must have fallen asleep because I woke up in the middle of the night and had to sneak back into the house like a ghost.

CHAPTER 7

The next morning I brought a bucket of oats to Sugar Pie in the back pasture before breakfast. I was brushing her down when Bee appeared.

"Yesterday, at Treva's, you felt it, didn't you?" she asked. "Your gift."

I kept brushing Sugar Pie. I wanted to tell her that I'd felt it even before that. I wanted to tell her about all I'd found up on Solace Hill, everything. But I also didn't want to talk about it right now.

"Some of Harlan's cigarette butts were out under the peach trees," I said. I did want her to know that. Know what might be coming our way and what it might mean.

She was quiet a moment. "You think he's here?" she asked. She was testing me, seeing how much

I felt and knew. I turned away and ran the brush down Sugar Pie's belly. I couldn't give her an answer to something I didn't know myself.

"No," she said finally, with a hint of relief that caught me off guard. "I don't feel him here. He's not here."

But you paid for his bail in Louisiana a month ago, didn't you?

Miss Lilah's geese appeared at the fence, honking. Bee clapped her hands at them, and they waddled off.

"You told me once you didn't feel him no more, that he was too far away," I said. I leaned my face into Sugar Pie's neck.

"I don't know if I *ever* felt him," Bee said gently. "He never really seemed a part of me, of any of us. Even as a child your daddy was always a wanderer. I could barely keep him corralled."

"But he's my father," I said quietly. "Bo's and mine, even though he's not a good one."

Bee snorted.

"Did you pay his bail, Bee?" I asked.

"I thought'd you'd been in my room," she said. "I

didn't pay it. We simply don't have the money. And if we did, well, I can't tell you if I would have."

Something rushed through me then, sadness maybe that he could still be sitting in jail? No, disappointment that Bee'd have to make a decision like that. And shame, deep shame that Bee could leave her own son sitting there, even if she had no choice.

"June Rain thinks he's coming home," I mumbled into Sugar Pie, my eyes starting to sting. "That's why she's perked up."

"June Rain thinks lots of things that aren't true, Esme."

"Maybe someday I'll find out what *is* true about her. She's my mama, after all."

"I don't think she fully understands that she's your mama and Bo's, too," said Bee. "Harlan should've never brought her here. . . . She's—"

"I don't want to talk about this," I told her angrily. I didn't want to hear her grown-up talk. That's how she always talked to me, even when I was Bo's age. I wanted to ask when I'd fill out my bra, and I wanted to tell her how deep down I wished I could have a new pair of jeans from Dallas—things a twelve-year-old girl wants to talk about.

I glanced over to her, and her eyes softened, but I knew she wouldn't say she was sorry. Those were words that would never come from Bee McCauley. Never in a million years.

"We having eggs this morning?" I asked.

"How'd you know that?" She sounded surprised.

I pulled a bit of eggshell out of her hair and held it up. She actually smiled a little before she turned to leave. "Anything I need to know about those hens, Esme? They been producing half what they usually do. Did Old Jack get in the henhouse?"

"Maybe," I answered. "But what do I need to know? What is it you want me to know?"

I could see her running it all over in her mind, then she spoke. "It's the seen and unseen, Esme. You got to know them both inside and out, and which is which, and more importantly, what's in-between. It's the art of finding a heartbeat in the darkness a mile away, a dragonfly wing at the bottom of a river. You'll know it when you're close, Esme. You'll know."

I felt a sweet shiver go down my spine, a

connection to my grandma even if it was a tiny, tender thread that made me feel all strange inside. "Who'll tell me?" I whispered.

But she'd already turned for the house, and I knew without a doubt that there was more, much more to that puzzle.

Bee and Old Jack had gone to take June Rain to the Just Teasin.' Sweetmaw said June Rain done real good with the perms and comb-outs and wanted her back today. Bee and Sweetmaw had even talked on the phone for a minute or two. I'd heard Bee praising June Rain for her hard work, hoping June Rain was back in a good spell. But I knew from experience not to trust good spells, 'cause the bad ones always came back, and came back stronger.

I was picking peaches when I found something peculiar in one of the oldest trees in the orchard. It was a chain of little paper girls with clasped hands. It was wrapped around several limbs like a garland around a Christmas tree. A friendship chain. Dovie must have spent a long time making it. I watched Bo dash across the yard blowing Finch's bubbles. Sugar Pie was in her enclosure lazily chomping on some daisies. I gently pulled the chain down and held it to my heart.

An hour later, when Bee had taken June Rain to town, I'd picked all the ripe peaches I could and neatly lined the baskets up in the barn. I ran upstairs to wash up and change out of my dusty coveralls. June Rain's Maybelline mascara, recently unearthed from somewhere, was on the counter. I looked up at my eyes in the mirror. I had Harlan's green eyes, but they were like saucers with ghostly lashes—"bug's wings," Bee politely called them. I quickly slashed a little bit of the mascara on my invisible lashes and rubbed some lipstick on. I stood back and couldn't believe what I saw—my eyes looked pretty, well, almost pretty.

I hovered outside Bee's room, then listened carefully at her door. I went in and retrieved the telegram from the bureau drawer—I glanced at it. The phone number for the jail was there. I snuck down the stairs as quietly as I could and loaded Bo on the back of my bicycle. "Why do you look like a raccoon?" Bo asked. I ignored him and we headed over to Finch's house.

Finch was sitting on his sagging porch whittling a stick. An open book lay next to him. He'd probably been reading like he always does. If he was whittling a stick that meant he was pondering, savoring what he'd just read.

I wondered if Granger had said anything to Finch about us finding him and the moonshine. I doubted it. Finch looked up and smiled. As I walked closer, I saw he was wearing a new pair of jeans, a popular kind that flare at the bottom. And a new pair of shoes, too, moon boots, and one of those necklaces with the shark's tooth on a leather cord. A shiver ran down my back as I stared at that tooth, thinking about Louella Goodbones up on Solace Hill.

"Where'd you get those?" I asked, my eyes shooting away from the tooth, down at his boots. Bo ran back and forth across the porch swan diving into the Aberdeens' porch swing.

"Granger bought them for me," he said proudly. They looked hot for summer and stupid, and worse than my white Mary Jane's. In the past I would've told him so, but something stopped me. Maybe it was thinking about how I'd last seen Granger, sitting on that log looking like he'd swallowed a bug.

"Where'd he get 'em, Finch?" I asked, getting a sinking feeling, my mind connecting things.

"He took me over to Paradise yesterday," he answered. "Said Hollis didn't deserve his hard-earned cash."

One of the Aberdeens' dogs came running around from the back of the house with a bird in his mouth. Bo cheerfully chased him around the yard.

I kicked at the dirt. "Did Granger say anything about me?" I asked casually.

Finch got up. "Granger? Why would Granger say something about you, Esme McCauley?" His face turned a little pale. He spit on the ground.

"No reason," I said, staring at the splat of spit, thinking that wasn't like Finch. It was more like his brother.

"Do you think he likes you or something?" he asked. He snorted. A strange feeling passed through me. Finch Aberdeen, my closest and oldest friend in the world, was *jealous*. Even if he had the wrong idea, he was jealous, and to my surprise I felt a tickle in my heart like a doodlebug had crawled across it.

He stood a little closer to me, looking straight into my eyes, and I noticed two little cuts on his chin.

"What's that smell?" he asked, crinkling his nose.

Oh, God, how I wished I'd worn the deodorant Bee gave me. He pointed at my lips.

"Oh, that," I said, embarrassed. The lip gloss. "It's Cherry Smash." I bit my lip.

"And you got something all over your eyes." He was looking at me funny.

"Well, you've shaved," I said. What a joke. He didn't even have peach fuzz yet.

"Granger got me a razor, too," he said, shrugging his shoulders.

Finch sat back down and picked up his whittling stick. I leaned on the porch rail, holding on to one of the paint-peeled columns. I looked down at his book. *Robinson Crusoe.* Finch loved books that took him on a journey, anywhere away from Hollis. Miss Ferriday sometimes ordered books from other libraries just for him.

He pulled a box of candy cigarettes out of his back pocket and offered them to me. I took two and shoved them in my mouth, feeling a little guilty knowing that they were probably bought with Granger's moonshining money.

I wanted to tell him about all my new secrets like Louella Goodbones, and what his brother Granger was up to in the woods, and that tingly-numbly feeling in my toes each time something wondrous happened, but I couldn't. It was all there on the tip of my tongue. But the words couldn't leave my lips.

After getting sundaes at Sonic, I took Bo down by the hardware store. While he ate his sundae, I slipped into the phone booth and put a quarter in the slot. I dialed the jail. After two rings, someone picked up.

"Sheriff's office. Sheriff Bennett," a faraway-sounding male voice said distractedly.

"Is Harlan McCauley in your jail there?" I whispered into the phone, like they do on TV in spy shows. I looked over my shoulder. Streams of chocolate were running down Bo's face as he hopped along the sidewalk, spinning his red spoon in his sundae.

"Harlan?" The sheriff laughed. "No, that

scoundrel's not here. Painted up the jail to pay for half his bail. Did a great job. Then hightailed it out of here several weeks ago."

"Who paid the other half?" I asked. "Sir." I wondered if Bee had come through after all.

"Some old feller passing through—he looked like Rumpelstiltskin. They seemed to know each other. Some lady called just as they were heading out, told me to tell Harlan she didn't have the money because she'd just buried his father." I pressed the phone tight up against my ear.

"You still there?" he asked.

"What did he say?" I sounded like I was squealing. "Harlan," I added, trying to disguise my voice again. *He knew.* He knew Paps had died and he hadn't come home.

"Didn't say anything, just waved that jolly wave of his and out they went." I hung up and grabbed Bo's hand. *He could be anywhere,* I told myself. Anywhere.

We spotted Bee around the corner outside Sweetmaw's talking to Rose Galloway, who was just leaving. Her hair was blown out and shiny. She flipped it over her shoulder when she saw me.

Bo ran up behind Bee and tried to crawl through her legs. She pulled him to his feet, frowning at me as she wiped his chocolaty face.

"So what do you need, Rose Galloway?" Bee asked, shoving her handkerchief back in the pocket of her jeans. My toes started to tingle and I already knew without a doubt what she wanted and where it was. Rose had a rare bird, a scarlet-chested parakeet her daddy'd bought her in Dallas. The parakeet was named Popsicle and she always trotted it out on Bring Your Pet to School day. It was now sitting on Vera Godly's fence, Vera's cat Panther ready to pounce on it.

It's the seen and unseen, Esme, and all that's in-between. And you have to use your gift when it comes to you. But I thought about all those mean names they'd been calling me all these years. Thumby, and Butthole Mouth, and Saucer Eyes.

"Popsicle's missing. Mama left the cage door open when she fed her this morning."

Bee frowned. She didn't know all about how the

kids at school treated me, but I think she guessed some of it, and she knew Rose Galloway was the worst. A worm is the only animal that can't fall down, Bee had once said about Rose when I'd begged for a new pair of Jordache jeans like the ones Rose wore. "You're supposed to be picking peaches," she said to me now. Her chin jutted out slightly, her spectacles sliding down her nose.

"I finished early," I said, turning away from her.

"I don't have time to go looking for a bird, Rose Galloway," Bee told Rose. What'd got in her crock?

I thought about that poor bird about to be crunched by Vera Godly's cat. "It's sitting on Vera Godly's fence," I said. "You'd better hurry, before it flies away or gets eaten."

Bee swung around to me. I turned my head so she couldn't see my nostrils flaring. "I saw it on my way over here, couldn't miss it," I lied as Rose started to run toward Vera's. "I'm going to the library, if that's okay."

"You swear you got those peaches picked?" Bee asked.

"Of course. They're in the barn."

"How many bushels?"

"Five half-bushel baskets."

"Well, all right then. You hurry on home afterward. We need to start the honey. I have orders already from a shop over in Paradise. And as soon as you're home, you're wiping all that dadgum gunk off your face."

The Hollis Public Library was a block off the town square, nestled behind a fringe of cottonwood trees. I found Miss Ferriday at her desk typing a letter. When old Mrs. Tivey died a few years back, Miss Ferriday showed up for the job all the way from Austin and set everyone's tongues a wagging as to why a pretty girl like her wasn't married yet.

"Esme McCauley," she said, surprised to see me. "What are you doing here, honey?" I wasn't known for my literary pursuits. I really wasn't known for anything at all.

"I was wondering . . . ," I began, my eyes flitting around, my nostrils flaring. But Miss Ferriday didn't even blink. I think she was used to people asking for books in a round-about way. "Do you have any books on . . . well . . ."

"Yes?"

"Big bones?" I finally blurted out.

Vera Godly and Lottie Broadway came through the front door then, arm in arm, and went toward the magazines. I could tell June Rain had done their hair; Vera's chignon looked like it was from Paris or something, and Lottie's permanent was just right.

"What do you mean by *big bones*?" Miss Ferriday asked.

"Like a big animal, old, ancient, giant, buried deep," I whispered. "Maybe a dinosaur, but I don't know."

"Oh, I see, you mean animal skeletons or fossils?" Miss Ferriday's eyes got big.

"You can't tell anyone, though," I pleaded. "Please."

She smiled. "Librarians don't tell," she said. "Ever." That was probably true. She probably knew more about people in Hollis than Bee did.

"Are there even dinosaurs *in* Texas?" I asked her. I felt stupid for asking, but I didn't know.

"I'll look, honey," she said, and soon she was

back and handing me a neat stack of books. One was called *Dinosaurs of America*. Another *Reptiles of North America*, *Ancient Monsters*. She'd slipped *Jane Eyre* into the middle of the pile. She handed me a grocery bag to put them in.

"We don't have anything on Texas dinosaurs specifically. But there might be something in those books. And maybe there'll be something on microfiche. The librarian at the Paradise Library, Mrs. Greenly, can look for us as well. I'll call her today and ask . . . and Esme?"

I nodded.

"It's our secret," she said. "Don't worry."

Suddenly Mady Whitshaw and Dovie Cade appeared next to me. Mady's mama Mabel had some crippling disease, had for years been hanging on by God's good graces, according to Bee. She'd recently turned for the worse and could hardly get out of bed. The medicine she needed to ease her pain was too expensive for their family to afford anymore.

"What secret?" Mady asked.

I grabbed the bag of books to my chest, suddenly embarrassed. Miss Ferriday saved me. "Esme is joining our summer reading program."

I stood there, my teeth clinched together. I looked up at Dovie and she smiled at me.

"My mother, out of the blue," Dovie paused, looking at me, "found Grandma's wedding ring. She is over the moon. She's going to sell it when it's time for me to go off to college."

I'd found the ring for Dee Dee all right, but I didn't know if I was ready to be Dovie's friend again. Mady pulled her away, then Dovie smiled at me over her shoulder as they went out the door.

I found a quiet corner in the reference section. I opened *Dinosaurs of America* and started flipping through the pages. I came to one drawing of a dinosaur with a long neck, its mouth open showing a row of sharp teeth. Allosaurus. I hoped Louella Goodbones looked like this—ancient, yet elegant and fierce—oh, how I hoped so. I got an excited, warm feeling as I turned through the pages, one by one, looking into those ancient eyes.

I ran straight up to Solace Hill. Bee looked out from the peach trees where she was picking, but I didn't care. I lay down under the tractor, the earth cooling me, like I was floating in sweet river water.

I looked at the quilt covering Louella. Paps had been so close to the bone when he'd passed away. *What was it, Paps? What were you looking for?* Bump joined me, scrambling over my arm and on down to a muddy rut made by the tractor wheels. He sat atop something that had a hard smooth edge and was not meant to be here.

I rolled over to it, and Bump hopped off. I ran my finger down its length. Hard, like wood. Was it part of Louella? My stomach dropped as I dug more dirt away, more and more till I was able to pull it out. It was a small embossed wooden box. With a bee carved on top.

I carefully opened it. There was a small gold coin. *A gold coin.* I sensed a shadow over the tractor and a deep gloom passed through me. The gold coin suddenly burned in my palm. *Don't touch!* I quickly put it back and covered the box with dirt again.

Where was the other coin? The one Paps had found? Or was this it? Bee, so good at finding things, was even better at hiding them.

I crawled out from the tractor and knelt down next to Louella Goodbones, running my fingers up and down her exposed skull.

Bee called for me from the orchard just then, startling me so I fell over and rolled a little down the hill. I just kept going and going, somersaulting like Finch and I'd done as little kids. I dusted myself off at the bottom and ran the rest of the way.

I woke up with a start. It was still pitch-black. Something was stirring, a creak, a hush, a stilled footstep, the telltale sounds that mean someone else is awake. Bo had gotten into my bed sometime in the night, like he often did. I peeled away his arm, and put his hand, clutching a plastic soldier, across his chest. Then I tiptoed out of the room, making my own unintended squeaks.

It was June Rain. She was sitting at her window. I stood in the doorway and she glanced back at me, her tear-streaked face dusted silver in the moonlight.

"I had an uncle who came to visit us once. Tall as a timber tree, with a long beard down to his belly button, like a wooly mammoth," she whispered. "One night he passed out in the yard and a bird built a nest in his beard. Can you believe that? Everywhere he went the bird went, too, sitting on those eggs. We named him Uncle Hen. And one day the eggs hatched."

"What happened to them?" I asked, mesmerized that she was telling me something about her family, even though it sounded made up like a fairy tale.

"They flew away," she said. "And the next day Uncle Hen left." She turned her head back to the window.

I wanted to tell her Harlan wasn't coming home. Bee would've seen it and told us if he was, I believed that with all my heart.

I stored Uncle Hen with the other clues—the ticket stub, the locket, the bubblegum dot snake bite scar, and all those secret postcards from Harlan. As I fell back to sleep, I pictured Uncle Hen under the revival tent, holding the hand of a little black-haired girl, as birds danced above.

CHAPTER 8

I helped Bee make breakfast— buttermilk biscuits with gravy and we were going to have Bo's favorite, one-eyed Milly's, an egg on a piece of toast and fried up in a skillet. June Rain was still asleep. I'd peeked into her room and she was buried completely under the covers like a prairie dog hiding from a storm.

Bee had sent Bo to collect eggs from the chickens, but I could see him in the peach trees hopping around with a stick between his legs, Old Jack running behind.

"Bee," I said. So much was on my mind, swirling around like one big tornado, and I didn't know if I could hold it all in.

"What is it, Esme?" she asked as she turned

the oven on, then gave it a horse kick. "Spit it out, honey."

"Why haven't I ever called June Rain *Mama* and Harlan *Daddy*?" I asked. I surprised myself that I asked her this, when there was so much more ready to spill out. Bee says sometimes the heart winnows things down to their simplest. She stopped stirring the creamed gravy. I glanced out the window and saw Bo throwing peaches at Old Jack, who was trying to catch them. Bo didn't call June Rain *Mama* either, and Harlan was never around long enough to be called anything, I suppose.

"You came out like you were already grown-up, Esme McCauley, even though you were half as big as a minute. I looked into those green eyes of yours and it was like you'd already seen the whole world but were still looking for something. You never were like a baby, so serious you were. Maybe that's why I always treated you the way I did. You seemed to expect it."

"What was it like the day I was born?" I asked. No one ever talked about it, not really.

Bee resumed stirring in a slow, steady rhythm,

like she was picking her words. "Well, it was like any day," she said, and I frowned.

She peered over her glasses at me and added, "Any day a baby is born is a beautiful day." But I knew she didn't mean it. There was a hollowness in her voice. A honeycomb hollow.

I thought about when Bo was born, Harlan leaving, Bee slapping him. And June Rain having the biggest smile I'd ever seen. This baby was good, this baby was whole, finished.

"Yours was a difficult birth. June Rain was in labor for thirty-six hours. We were all worried. Especially Homer. June Rain howled like a wolf for hours on end. And you were just so early, so early. They'd never seen a baby that early in Paradise."

"Then what happened?"

She looked at me but didn't answer.

"Well, where was Harlan?" I asked. I knew there was more to the story, some sadness tucked in.

Bee looked serious now. "He was outside smoking cigarettes. He was there, though." She turned back to the stove and I wondered if her own nostrils were flaring. Or if Harlan really *had* been there. We worked for a while in silence. Somewhere in the distance Sugar Pie neighed.

"But why don't I call her *Mama*?" I asked again after a few minutes. I couldn't help myself. I'd never been a pot stirrer, but now I was and it felt right digging it all up. Bee often says some skeletons are better off staying buried. Little did she know.

"I guess you thought June Rain was such a beautiful name, so why not use it?" Bee said.

I started plopping the biscuit dough out on a baking sheet. Bee was sugaring everything up, not quite telling me the truth. I knew it and she knew it.

"*June Rain*. No one has a name like that round here. Where'd she get such a name?" *Plop. Plop.* "Where'd she come from?"

"You know. Harlan brought her home from the revival tent."

"Yes, but before that," I said. *Plop.* "You know I mean before that."

"Don't know," Bee said flatly. "Don't suppose we'll ever know. Let it go, Esme."

"But what if she goes back to wherever she came from?" I asked.

"Is that what you're afraid of, Esme?"

I didn't answer, feeling a sting in my eyes.

"She's not going anywhere."

"How do you know that?" I asked. I thought about how many times I'd looked under June Rain's bed, praying that suitcase hadn't moved, watching her every minute, watching her as she sat so still I thought she'd turn to stone.

"She doesn't have anywhere to go."

A tear ran down my face, knowing that the delicate thread that kept her here was only because she had nowhere else to go, and not because of us.

Later that afternoon a big shiny Cadillac sped up the drive, a cloud of dust around it. It was coming with bad news, I could feel it. Old Jack felt it, too. He ran around the house barking, then started pawing at the kitchen door. Bee had just come back from taking June Rain to Just Teasin'. She glanced out the door, her mouth pinching into a frown. The car disappeared from view as it pulled around the side of the house.

There was a knock on the front door. We never

used the front door. Bo came bursting into the family room. "It's Mr. Galloway from the bank!" he said. "Look what he brought me!" He was clutching a little metal coin box in the shape of a cash register with "Hollis Grand National Bank" printed on it. Rose Galloway's father, the bigwig banker of Hollis, stood in the doorway.

"You take Bo outside, Esme," said Bee. "Out the kitchen door. And bring Old Jack with you. I'll take care of this."

I pushed Old Jack and Bo out the kitchen door and told Bo he'd better go pick up all the peaches he'd been throwing around earlier before Bee saw the mess. Then I crawled under the house. I wrapped my arms around my legs, rested my chin on my knees, and I listened. First there was just footsteps. Then the hollow echo of voices. The words came down to me like falling cinders—hushed, and murky, and sizzling.

At first I could only hear snippets, things like "mortgage," and "payment," and "soon," words that mimicked that torn-up letter. Each time Mr. Galloway said something, Bee's voice got a little louder, like someone was turning up the volume on the TV, while Mr. Galloway's got softer and softer. Then more words floated down, "letter" and "Homer" and "bad times."

"You have no right to come to my home! Get out!" That was loud and clear.

And then Mr. Galloway was saying, "You have two months, Mrs. McCauley. Two months. Nothing is going to change between now and then. It's best you start accepting that." I knew no amount of peach picking or jars of honey was going to fix this.

A moment later the front door slammed. I crawled out from under the house, wiping off my rear end as Mr. Galloway drove his big Cadillac away.

Later I went out to the orchard and crushed peach leaves, letting the pieces fall to the ground. Old Jack lay by my side, swatting away horseflies with his tail. Bee says horseflies are the most persistent; they don't give up no matter what, not like the fireflies who leave and never come back.

"It's all right, boy," I said, patting his head. "It's

all right. Come on, let's go." Old Jack lifted his head then, as though he understood my thoughts, his wet, gray eyes boring into mine.

I retrieved the pickax and shovel, then Old Jack and I climbed Solace Hill. I very carefully picked away more earth from around the skull, the dried mud clots coming off easily, the layer beneath thicker and stubborn. I could see more of her head now, four teeth, even longer than the first, and the hollow sockets where her eyes had been. It was almost as though she was smiling. *What were you doing up on this hill, Louella Goodbones? So many* millions *of years ago? Did you fall down in the mud, get stuck and die? Were you a mama? Or just barely grown up, like me? Or were you old and just couldn't go any farther? Why'd you stop on our Solace Hill?*

And then all these millions of years later, my paps drove his tractor up here looking for something, perhaps a carved box with a bee on it. I lay back on the cool earth, closed my eyes, and started to drift off. I didn't notice Bump when he ran across Louella Goodbones's head. Neither did Old Jack, who was snoring now under the tractor on Bee's crazy quilt.

"Well, what in the blue wonder is *that*?"

Finch! I cussed under my breath, sure I was saying some words worse than what got Bee kicked out of Women's Missionary Quilting Club.

"What in the heck are you doing up here, Finch?" I shrieked.

He ignored me and walked closer to Louella Goodbones, his mouth open in a big giant O. His mouth was apparently full of Pop Rocks because they all shot out on top of Louella Goodbones. The smell of sugary grape wafted through the air. I wanted to slap him good. How dare he spy on me and follow me up here. How dare he!

"I've been worried about you, Esme. You've been acting so strange," he said, still staring at the skull.

"Get out of here," I said, tears springing to my eyes. "Get of here!" It was all ruined. The only secret I had in the world and now it was ruined. By Finch Aberdeen, of all people, my only friend.

"Why didn't . . . why didn't you tell me? Why did

you keep something like this from me?" he asked, his voice catching.

"'Cause," I said. "'Cause . . ." I couldn't finish. I felt terrible.

"This is big, Esme. Really big, do you know that?" He was leaning down now, practically touching her. "Is it some sort of dinosaur skull?" he said, looking over at me incredulously. He sat back on his haunches, stunned.

"It's mine, Finch Aberdeen. And mine alone." I stood with my hands on my hips.

He frowned. "You don't think I know that? Who do you think I am, Esme McCauley?"

I looked down, ashamed, remembering all we'd done for each other our whole lives. The times I'd hidden Finch under our house when his daddy came home drunk, the times he'd cheer me up after Harlan left, the time he pulled the paper off my back, how really we had no other friends at school but each other.

"Do you remember that big rain we had a few days ago?" I asked, and he nodded. "It brought part of her up. Then I started digging." I didn't want to tell him it was really Paps who'd started it all, and then a ghost, or maybe not a ghost, in the henhouse, and then the fireflies leading Bo and me up the hill. I could keep all of that to myself. He'd think I was crazy for feeling like it was all threaded together somehow like one of Bee's crazy quilts.

"What are you going to do with it, Esme?" he asked.

"I don't know yet," I told him. "I'm just trying to see what she looks like."

"You think there's more down there?" He brushed a little more dirt from her jaw.

"Yeah," I said. "Yeah, there's more. Lots more." My toes started to tingle. There *was* lots more of her down there waiting to be found. Those bones were vibrating up through my toes, my legs, all the way up. Even my ears were tingling now, and I wondered if Finch could see them move.

Then I noticed something. "Where are your new boots?"

"They looked stupid in the summer."

He was right. It felt good to laugh. I held out my hand. "Pop Rocks, please."

He reached in his back pocket and handed me the packet. I dumped them all in my mouth, the whole packet.

"You're not going to tell, are you, Finch?" The candy was exploding around in my mouth like tiny firecrackers.

"No, Esme. I'm not going to tell. Not ever."

And I knew then he wouldn't. Finch Aberdeen would never tell.

Finch returned after dinner and helped me dig for hours, neither of us saying one word. Then he disappeared back home in the moonlight. I stopped briefly to put the tools away in the storm cellar. Bee was sitting there in the living room, silent, smoking on a cigar again, when I went inside.

"What you been doing up there on that hill?" she asked. There it was. She'd finally asked.

"Planting a little garden for Paps," I knew she couldn't see my nostrils, but they were flaring all right.

"Nothing good has ever come from that hill," she whispered.

I thought about the carved box, the bee. Something told me she would not tell me a thing if I asked about it.

"Maybe," I said finally. "But maybe all those bad things are gonna add up to something good. Something good has to come eventually, Bee. That's what I think."

"I don't know, Esme." She took a puff on the cigar. I knew she was thinking of those honeycomb sorrows, one after another, one after another. But I wasn't going to think of all the sad things that had happened to us. Not now. I couldn't.

"'Bout time we sell that damn tractor," she said. "We need the money."

"No one is going to want it," I said quietly. "It's practically rusted out." My heart lurched. It'd be like taking Paps away all over again if she sold it.

"Go on upstairs, then, go to bed," Bee said. "Been staying out awfully late, haven't you?"

I ran upstairs and shut my door. When I got into bed, I opened *Dinosaurs of America*. A small folded-up news clipping fell out. It was an article about a professor at Southern Methodist University in Dallas who had dug all around Texas looking for dinosaurs.

His name was T. Rex Abramanov, and there was a grainy photo of him standing on a rocky ledge, one booted foot out, a tool belt with sharp, shiny tools around his waist, his angular face shadowed under a weathered safari hat. *Abramanov.* I'd never heard of a name like that around Hollis. "Abramanov." I said it aloud, letting it roll off my tongue, like something new yet delicious. He looked like he'd just stepped out of a movie. I'd studied all the library books, but couldn't find anything that looked exactly like my Louella Goodbones. I wondered if someone like T. Rex Abramanov would know who she was. I fell asleep dreaming of faraway lands and ghosts walking up and down Solace Hill.

CHAPTER 9

The next morning Finch showed up at the door with a garden shovel as big as Texas and I had to push him back down the kitchen steps and march him into the orchard. I looked back at the house. Bee was watching from the kitchen window. "We can't dig now, Finch, not now. Bee knows something's up."

"Of course she does," said Finch. "She's Bee McCauley. And maybe it's good she knows. Maybe everyone should know. I've been doing some thinking. Those bones up there might be worth a lot of money."

"Seriously?" I hadn't thought of it that way. I hadn't really imagined what could happen.

"Maybe. We should have someone come and

look at it, Esme," he said. "I think it's gonna make you famous."

"But I don't want to be famous, Finch," I said. "And I'm not ready to share her with anyone." But it did make my mind start spinning around and around, that maybe Bee was wrong and I was right. Maybe all the sorrows on Solace Hill *could* add up to something really good.

A moment later Bee hollered for me to come in and help with the honey.

"Can I come, too?" Finch asked.

I looked at him funny. Something was up. "You want to help bottle the honey?"

"Don't want to go home is all."

I didn't ask more. He'd tell me later if he wanted to.

We spent the whole morning helping Bee pour honey through funnels into jars. Even June Rain and Bo helped, although I think Bo got more on his fingers than into the jars. Old Jack sat next to him, drooling, waiting for each sweet drip that oozed off the side of the table. Every now and then Bo put his hand down and Old Jack licked away.

Harlan used to paint the labels, a cute little

bumble bee at the bottom below the name, *Bee's Honey*. But since he'd been gone, Bee'd had them printed over in Paradise. I saw June Rain linger over one of the labels, knowing just what she was thinking, and I think everyone else did, too.

"Didn't Harlan used to paint the labels?" Finch asked, and I kicked him. June Rain pushed her chair back from the table and walked off. Grief shades people in different ways. Harlan was painted all over us, and there was no way to wash it off.

Later I begged Bee to let Bo and me go into Hollis with June Rain while she went to deliver some of the honey orders in Paradise. She agreed and dropped us at Just Teasin'. June Rain and Bo headed into the beauty parlor, but I told them I'd catch up later. I waited for the Bee Wagon to round the corner off Main, and when I saw the last of the little white curtains, I ran as fast as I could to the library.

Miss Ferriday got a big grin on her face when she saw me. "I heard from Mrs. Greenly. She sent over five more books on dinosaurs! And one on Texas dinosaurs," Miss Ferriday said, opening the book up. "It seems most of them were found all the way down in Big Bend." She pointed to a map of Texas, way down in the tippy corner where several different dinosaurs were drawn as though they were walking across the desert. "But a row of dinosaur footprints was once found in Glen Rose about an hour from here." She pointed to the top of the map where we were in North Texas.

"Footprints. But no dinosaur, no big dinosaur skeleton, ever found round here?"

She shook her head. "But footprints, Esme. That means they were here. And maybe they're just waiting to be found."

She stacked the books in a bag for me and a few minutes later I left, proudly swinging the bag.

I rushed into the Just Teasin', the smell of permanents, fruity shampoos, and hair spray stinging my eyes. Sweetmaw had decorated the Just Teasin' in fifty shades of pink. It looked like one big powder puff of cotton candy, with shiny black salon chairs topped by hot pink dryers.

"Well, what's up your craw, young lady?"

Sweetmaw said, glancing up from rolling Lottie Broadway's hair that was thin and pale as a spider-web, two strands on each roller.

"Huh?" asked Lottie, her hand up to her ear. Sweetmaw whispered something to her that made her giggle and turn red. Sweetmaw, as sweet as she is, tells off-color jokes. It's the only thing I can think of in the whole world that links them, those two sisters; otherwise they are like night and day—Bee gloomy as a pocket, and Sweetmaw light as the sun.

Vera Godly was asleep under one of the hair dry-ers and June Rain was papering Violet Galloway's hair, preparing it for a perm. June Rain hadn't noticed me yet, but Mrs. Galloway had. She looked over her glasses at me, with a small strained smile, the kind of smile people usually gave me, but then it widened. "Thank you," she mouthed. "For Popsicle."

I blinked. I didn't know what to say. I wondered if she knew about her husband's trip to our farm.

Bo was playing on the floor with his soldiers, who were launching an attack. I plopped down in one of the empty chairs and pawed through the *Glamour* magazines, trying to get my mind off what Finch had said about showing Louella Goodbones to someone.

Sweetmaw was telling a story about a friend whose husband night fishes when he's been on a bender. Vera Godly's eyes popped open. Violet Galloway snapped her magazine up in front of her like she wasn't listening. "Well, he caught a 'throwback,' meaning the fish wasn't worth keeping, but it was so cute he brought it up to his lips to kiss it—and then he suddenly heard some wailing and thought perhaps it was the drowning woman. And the next thing he knew that fish jumped right down his throat and got stuck. True-itt had to take him to the hospital in Paradise to get it taken out. Ten stitches later and he still swears he heard something in the river."

Then suddenly Finch's mama Pearl Mae was there, holding the door open with her foot, like she wasn't staying long. I don't think Pearl Mae had *ever* stepped into the Just Teasin'. She'd tried to do something with her hair, though, teasing it up in the back like Sweetmaw's, but it looked like humps on a camel. She had on her church dress—an old quilted cotton that frayed at the hem.

Sweetmaw looked over at her, and everyone else did, too. "Can I help you, Pearl Mae?" she asked, her eyebrows rising.

I could see Pearl Mae's chest heaving, her eyes were big like she was about to cry. She looked at me a moment and opened her mouth. But then whatever she was gonna say left her. She pushed the door with her foot and slipped away.

"Well, I'll be," said Sweetmaw.

Everyone knew that gossip spreads faster at her beauty parlor than bad news at a funeral, especially if Vera Godly was there.

Suddenly Vera Godly pointed at me. "My, she'd have to stand on her toes to look a rattler in the eye, June Rain. When she gonna start to grow up?" My heart sank. June Rain froze, the bottle of waving lotion she was holding poised in midair. "And maybe you could do something with her hair to hide those ears."

June Rain walked over to Vera Godly and started squirting the waving lotion all over her hair, the odor of ammonia filling the salon. I couldn't believe it, my quiet ghost of a mama, the mama who never did anything but exist, had poured the entire bottle out onto Vera's head!

I grabbed Bo's hand and told them I was taking him for ice cream. Sweetmaw gave me some money from the cash register and patted my back as we went out the door.

Much later, I stood in the doorway of Paps's room. The moonlight streamed through his window. Bee had left everything just the way it was the day he'd died, just like she'd left that tractor up on Solace Hill. But I was glad because it meant he was still here with us, in some small way. His room was on the first floor, across from the front parlor, far away from everyone else because he snored louder than a freight train, complete with the whistle, and it had vibrated through the whole house. Until Paps died, I hadn't realized how much his snoring soothed me, soothed all of us. About a week after Paps died, Bo had come in my room in the middle of the night screaming "Where is he, where is he? I can't feel the freight train." He wasn't able to sleep till June Rain put a cassette player next to his bed that played a tape of the sound of ocean waves over and over.

I lingered in Paps's doorway a long time, wanting to go in, but not able to move. I thought about the bee box and the gold coin and the mystery of it. My heart ached, but I sensed that by stepping over the threshold I might find something I wasn't ready for. Finally, I dashed in, grabbed his spectacles off the nightstand, and dashed out as quickly as I could.

And then just after I'd fallen asleep that night, I was sure Paps's snoring had jarred me awake. But I realized it was that vibrating feeling again. It was rising from my toes, up through my legs, circling around my knees, then spreading through my insides, twirling around like a fairy casting spells with her wand, till finally it worked its way back down to my fingertips. I lay there a long time with the wonder of it, scared but excited at the same time.

I stepped out into the yard, out into the peach trees, feeling as though I was walking in a dream. The moon shone brightly, so brightly the peaches gleamed like orangey jewels. Cicadas and crickets called to one another. I snapped a small branch off, like I'd done many times for Bee. But this time it was for me. I bent the branch down the middle, turned, and let it lead me. I went past the house, through the orchard, and into the woods, feeling as though the moon lit my way and protected me. At first I thought I was going to the hives, but the witching stick suddenly veered to the left and off I went deeper into the woods.

And then I was at a clearing at the edge of Bitter Creek. The witching stick tilted down, and I felt the power in it fade away. *So I found water!* I laughed. Water that I already knew was there. But suddenly the hair stood up on my arms and I saw something in the water to my left. I narrowed my eyes, trying to decipher what it was. Then the moon, high in the sky, danced across the creek, lighting up a figure. A bare-backed man, swimming across the creek.

I stepped back, quietly, ever so quietly, and stumbled on something. I looked down and saw it was a boot. I caught a glimpse of spatters of colorful paint, before I turned and ran. *Harlan's rainbow boots.* Only one person had boots like that. But why was I running from my father? Something inside me had told me to. *Run! Run as fast as you can!*

I woke up before dawn. I lay in bed a moment listening to the birds, thinking about what I'd seen the night before. Had I dreamed it? I got out of bed and went to the window. In the distance I could see a tiny pinprick of light shining, and a shiver went through me as I thought of Lilah's story about the ghost who floated up and down the hill.

I threw on my clothes and snuck out into the dawn. As I walked closer and closer so Solace Hill, I could see it was a lantern light and I got mad, mad, mad that someone was trespassing on my hill. But it was just Finch. He'd been picking away at Louella Goodbones. Bump, the traitor, was sitting on top of the lantern watching him.

"You look like you've seen a ghost." He looked worried.

"I think . . . I think I saw my father last night," I said, breathing hard. I wasn't mad anymore. Another feeling was seeping up through me. Fear. "But I don't know."

"Where?" he asked.

"Swimming across Bitter Creek," I said. I sat down next to him and Louella Goodbones, feeling like I was going to faint. I was so tired, so, so, tired. I listened to the chorus of birds, waiting for their sound to soothe me, but something was off.

"Maybe you were dreaming," said Finch.

I glanced over at Louella Goodbones. Almost half her skull was exposed now. A whole row of pointy teeth glinted in the soft light like she was smiling, as though she was glad we had found her and were releasing her from the deep dark earth.

"Maybe," I said. I hoped so. But the boots. The rainbow boots. I knew I hadn't dreamed up those.

I drifted off to the *click-clack* of Finch's shovel and the songs of the birds. I was back at the creek, watching the man swim across the water. He turned, mid-stroke, his smile glinting white in the moonlight. It was Harlan. Then I was running through the woods. *You missed something! Go back! You missed something!*

I opened my eyes.

"Shhhhh." I held my fingertip to my lips and looked up at Finch. "Shhhhh." He stopped digging and we both listened, still as statues. And then I realized what it was. It was the low, quiet wail of an animal.

CHAPTER 10

As Finch and I ran down the hill, I wondered if I'd heard that little cry all night and just not perceived it. Finch pointed to a white blanket with tiny red ladybugs on it, tented up over something. A mewling squeal came from beneath it.

"What is it?" Finch whispered

I took a deep breath and pulled back the blanket. It was a baby pig in a basket with a wide handle. The pig was wrapped loosely in a gray-blue blanket, its head peeking out. We stared at it, not knowing what to do. The pig's cries were crystal clear now and piercing. Finch took a step back.

"Lord almighty!" he said.

I leaned down, picked the piglet up, and clumsily held it to my chest. It was cold. Why would someone leave a brand-new baby piglet out here?

"How long were you up there, Finch?" I asked. "Did you see anyone?"

He shook his head no, his eyes focused on the blanket. "Couple of hours," he finally managed to mumble. "It's cute as a button, isn't it?"

"We better take it inside," I said, and started to walk fast as I could, then realized Finch wasn't behind me.

I continued toward the house, glancing back a few times at Finch, who was carrying the basket as though it would break. He finally caught up with me. We made it to the kitchen door just as Bee came down the steps, tying her robe, her hair billowing around her head.

"What in blue blazes are you doing out this early?" she asked, her eyes aflame. I saw a witching stick down by her side. She knew something needed to be found, but for some strange reason, I'd found it first. Old Jack appeared, his nose pressed into the screen door. Sometimes a dog just knows when to keep quiet.

I held out the baby piglet. It had fallen asleep,

perhaps lulled by my racing heartbeat. Bee looked down at it.

"Well, my goodness" was all she managed to say as she quickly took the baby piglet from my arms. I looked up to see June Rain standing in the kitchen behind Old Jack, her face in the shadows.

Finch and I gathered around Bee, looking down at the piglet. "Poor thing is shivering. It needs its mama," said Finch.

"Where did you find it?" Bee asked, turning to take the piglet into the house. I glanced down at the basket we'd found it in. It was expensive look-ing, like something they'd sell at Dyer's department store in Paradise. Then, peering closer, I saw a silk scarf tied to the base of the handle. It had roses all over it. *Rose.*

"At the bottom of Solace Hill," I said. I wondered if she'd ask what we'd been doing there, both of us, in the early morning.

"Esme, I think there's an old bottle of Bo's in the pantry. Put some milk to warm on the stove."

The baby piglet had started to mew and snort again. I quickly set to work, filling the bottle with the warm milk a minute later. I handed it to Bee. She pressed the bottle to the pig's snout and it quickly started sucking, the noise filling the whole kitchen. "This is one of those expensive miniature pigs people use as pets," Bee said, peering down at a face so ugly it was cute: white, sprinkled with soft black polka dots, with little beady black eyes.

Then June Rain held out her hands. Bee and I looked at her in wonder. June Rain took a step toward us. Finally Bee handed her the baby piglet and the bottle. June Rain, with the piglet in her arms like a newborn, turned and floated upstairs. And I couldn't help but think, that piglet was hardly bigger than a shoe, like I'd been.

I lay back in my bed a few hours later, listening for that piglet, but I couldn't hear anything. I crept down the stairs and peeked in the kitchen. Apparently Bee had already gone to the store, probably the Walmart in Paradise, which opened early. There was a big box of baby formula on the counter and preemie diapers. June Rain sat at the table, the piglet in her arms. My stomach turned a little.

"Did June Rain ever hold me back when you snatched me home?" I'd asked Bee once.

"Of course she did, Esme. A mama always holds her baby," she'd replied.

But I didn't think so.

Bo was kneeling on the chair next to June Rain, looking into the piglet's face. Old Jack was under the table, his ears slunk low.

Bee was on the phone. "I can't think who'd have left it—the last thing I found was not anything anyone would pay me for."

I thought about how I'd saved Rose Galloway's bird. Rose was the only one with an allowance, only one who could buy such a pet.

"Anyway, you'll just have to come over and get it," Bee continued, "at least come and see it, it's the cutest thing ever . . . but it's gonna have to go to a shelter." Five minutes later, Sweetmaw's pink Buick came roaring up the drive.

The screen door flung open with a *whap*! Sweetmaw walked right over to June Rain and peered down at the bundle in her arms. "My lord," Sweetmaw gushed. "Is that not the most darling thing ever? But it's gonna have to go to the animal shelter. Bee's right. That thing is gonna need constant care." She reached out her arms to hold it. June Rain pretended she didn't notice and kept on feeding it.

"June Rain," Bee said quietly.

June Rain held the piglet even closer. Bee and Sweetmaw exchanged looks.

"Best not come in for a few days, honey," Sweetmaw said to June Rain. "Vera Godly's madder than a wet hen. Gotta wait for it all to die down, and her hair to grow back. She's got a bald spot bigger than the moon and had to order a wig from Dallas, thanks to you." *And you*, I smiled to myself, thinking of how Sweetmaw hadn't stopped it.

"Well then, I'll be taking care of the baby anyway," said June Rain quietly.

Bee and Sweetmaw exchanged another glance.

"Well, I best be going," Sweetmaw said in an overbright voice. And then that piglet started to wail.

June Rain scooted away from the table and

calmly walked outside, the piglet cradled in the crook of her arm.

"Do we get to keep it?" Bo smiled. "June Rain wants her for us."

Old Jack came out from under the table, wagging his tail. A worry tickled across my heart. June Rain called it a *baby*, as though it were real. All that time I'd worried about June Rain's long drought, I just didn't realize it could be followed by a flood.

When Harlan was a little boy, he wandered away from home while Bee was picking peaches. He was there one moment swinging around the trunks of the trees, singing "Oh my darling, Oh my darling, Oh my darling Clementine!"—and gone the next. Bee says all it takes is an instant, and your child can disappear forever. But really Harlan's been dripping away from us like Bee's thick honey forever. Bee grabbed a witching stick and found him a half hour later at the beehives, mesmerized by their humming and darting.

I ran through the woods, my hair flying, my fingers tingling and tingling. *You missed something.*

You missed something. The image of June Rain, holding out her hands for that piglet, and Sweetmaw and Bee's worried looks flitted through my mind. I stopped, leaned against an oak tree to catch my breath. I snapped off a thin branch, bending it in the middle. It felt different than a peach tree witching stick.

I walked for a long while through the woods, letting the oak stick lead me, my trembling fingers barely holding it, my feet tingling more and more. Bitter Creek gurgled in the distance, and I knew I wasn't far from where I'd been last night. I startled some doves and they flew up into the trees cooing. My heart raced.

And then I came upon it. What I was supposed to find. A tiny cabin, squatting in a circle of maple trees. I approached slowly, as my witching stick lost its power, its hum dissipating, and pointed down low. I paused a moment before opening the door. I should have knocked, but I didn't.

Paintings. I knew them instantly. They were Harlan's. Harlan's "ain't-no-picture" paintings. And he'd even painted the walls. Everywhere June

Rain's face was peeking from the glops of paint, amidst flowers and hearts, and trees, and swirly-swirls. There was an easel with a half-finished painting propped on it. I walked over to it. Surprisingly, it was a painting of my face, my ears big and wide like Dumbo, flowers dancing out of them, my eyes big but beautifully rendered. I stifled a sob and pressed my finger to the paint. It was dry. I went around the room and touched the other paintings. They were all dry. Dry as dirt. He hadn't been here in a good long while.

But then I noticed a sleeping bag. That didn't mean anything, though. It could have been here forever. It didn't mean he was here now. He'd headed up north, that sheriff had told me. But June Rain's postcard was from Arizona, meaning he had skipped over Texas, skipping over us like he always did. I lingered in the cabin a long time, taking in his artwork, all that he'd done without us, in secret.

Then I stepped outside, shut the door, and walked home, my witching stick forgotten.

Later that afternoon I sat up on Solace Hill waiting for Finch. I sat next to Louella Goodbones trying to sketch her skull. Carefully I ran my fingers over every tooth, every groove and indentation, then sketched as best I could, adding arrows and notes about my observations, looking carefully at the different drawings of dinosaurs in the library books. I wanted to get Louella Goodbones just right. It had crossed my mind that the Professor Abramanov I'd seen in the newspaper clipping might know what she was, and maybe I'd send the drawings to him. But it made me sad to think she'd ever leave Solace Hill. So maybe I wouldn't send them.

Finch appeared, coming up the hill. He looked like he had been crying. He sat down next to me and peered over my shoulder. He actually smirked at my drawing, but it was nice to see him smile again at least.

"Here," he said quietly. "Let me finish her."

Finch could draw fine and perfect like an architect. One of his drawings of some sleek skyscraper in New York City once won a blue ribbon at the state fair. He took my pencil and notepad and started to erase and fix what I'd done, leaving the cartoony eyes. We smiled at each other, looking at those eyes; they resembled my big eyes a little and looked like the ones Harlan painted. We sat side by side for a long time as Finch's drawing beautifully came to life.

"What are you going to do with this?" he asked quietly. "After we finish it."

"I was thinking of sending it to that professor," I told him. "But I've changed my mind."

Suddenly Bump scurried off of Louella Goodbones and hopped under the tractor. Bee always said animals know things before we do. I stood up. Someone was coming up the hill. Old Jack bounded up to me, licking at my legs, as if he was apologizing, and then there was Bo right behind him.

"It's not fair, Esme," he said loudly in his not-in-church voice. "You're never in your bed anymore when I come to snuggle with you."

My eyes grew even bigger, my teeth clenched in a fake smile, hoping he'd look at me and Finch, hoping he wouldn't notice. But no. His eyes traveled down to the hillside and slowly, ever so slowly, over to Louella Goodbones, who looked like she was smiling in the semidarkness. Then he looked back at me.

"What is it?" he whispered in wonderment. "Is that what I think it is?"

I kneeled down in front of him, gently gripping his shoulders. "Yes, Bo. She's some kind of dinosaur and she's very special. But we must keep her secret for now."

A few minutes later we all went back home, Finch waving good-bye with the sketch tucked carefully in the dinosaur book under his arm.

CHAPTER 11

Later that morning June Rain took the piglet to work 'cause Bee said she wasn't going to take care of a pig; she had things to do, for God's sake. Vera Godly, wearing a scarf around her fried hair 'cause her wig hadn't arrived yet, had been telling everyone in Hollis about what June Rain had done and to stay away, but as soon as word spread about a fancy pig over at the Just Teasin', business perked up.

I paid a visit to the salon. There were ladies in every chair in various stages of getting their hair done, and three ladies cooing over the pig, who June Rain had dressed in baby clothes complete with a lacy bonnet tied under its chin. Every few minutes or so, someone would peer in the window, hand shielding eyes to get a better gander. I focused on the pig and realized they were *my* baby clothes, my incubator butter bean clothes.

"Now where did you say she came from?" someone hollered over their dryer.

Sweetmaw, who was on the phone, did one of those little waves, meaning she would answer in a minute, but had no intention of doing so. Miss Vera, not being one to miss such a spectacle, was hovering over the pig. She said, "Well, I guess it's cute; it's one of those expensive things that the movie stars buy, isn't it? Never seen one of them around here."

I thought the piglet was a little ugly now that I could see her in the light. Wouldn't be long before some sharp-eyed Hollis woman put two and two together and figured out that June Rain thought it was a real baby. Texas women aren't dumb. But maybe they'd play along for June Rain's sake. Maybe they knew this was what she needed.

"She should have one of those knitted caps for newborns, keep her head warm," Lottie Broadway offered with a nod.

"What's her name?" someone else asked.

Everyone peered at the piglet again, appraising

that little pink face and piggy snout under the lacy bonnet. The pig started to squeal and June Rain picked her up and patted her on the back. "Not sure yet," June Rain said. "Still thinking about it." The piglet whimpered.

"Put her back in her carrier where she feels warm," someone suggested.

"She's hungry, where's her bottle?" Miss Vera asked.

"Put some of Bee's honey in it. That'll calm her down."

"Honey's not good for a baby, has salmonella in it."

And then June started to sing, softly at first, then with a voice like a songbird and everyone, including the piglet, hushed, *Sweet child of mine, I'm going to let you shine.*

Sweetmaw bustled back to work, but I saw her discreetly wipe a tear away. Seeing June Rain like that, holding that piglet and knowing she never held me, or sang to me, made me really sad, too. Sometimes when we watched Saturday morning cartoons with Bo—me in front of her on the floor, she sitting in Paps's old chair—she would braid my hair. Those are the only times she's ever touched me. Sometimes I'd tell her I didn't like my braid pinched, so I could feel her fingers in my hair one more time.

"Her name is Jewell," June Rain suddenly proclaimed.

I walked out the door.

I rode my bike over to the Aberdeens' loaded up with a heavy basket. Finch must've been watching out the window because he came outside as soon as I walked onto their porch. The sweet cinnamony smell of Red Hots wafted in the air, but I didn't feel like asking Finch to share this time. I knew well enough to leave it alone. He pushed his glasses up and looked at me.

"What's that?" he asked, pointing at my basket.

"Peaches and honey, and Black Draught for Spoon, in case." Bee always made it when Spoon's been on a bender.

He looked away a moment, then bit his lip. "It's Granger," he said. "He's been missing. Daddy's sure he's gotten himself into some mess and that's why he's disappeared, and Mama keeps saying Granger's a good boy, doesn't get into trouble."

I swallowed hard, thinking maybe I should've told him about the moonshining business Granger was caught up in, and that's why he'd been giving Finch new money for candy and toys and ugly clothes. "How long's he been gone?" I asked.

"Since yesterday. He's been disappearing for a few hours here and there lately, but not usually overnight. Daddy doesn't want to call Sheriff Finney yet. He's hoping Granger will just show up on his own. He says he's gonna give him a whuppin' when he does. I think that's why Granger's lying low."

It was just like Finch to hope for the best. I had a feeling there was more to the story, and my toes vibrated for just a moment like a lawn mower being turned on then fluttering off.

"I'm real sorry to hear that," I said, shifting my weight, looking away from him. "You coming to help with the bones tonight?" I asked, and his face brightened.

"Yeah," he answered. "If I can sneak out."

"You finished the drawing?" I asked him.

"No," he said, looking away. "Still working on it. Might be a while."

Finch's mama called from inside the house somewhere, her voice weary. I handed him the provisions and he shut the door.

After dinner I knocked on June Rain's door. I found her in her usual spot, sitting by the window, the piglet sound asleep in the bassinet June Rain had brought down from the attic. I stood behind her, still as a statue. I thought about that piglet and how June Rain had sung to her and named her Jewell, a gem, a thing to be prized. Why wasn't I prized? Was it because I came too early and worried everyone? Was it because I was funny looking? Why did June Rain even stay with us—why didn't she go back to her own family?

"Been looking through my things, Esme?" June Rain asked, still facing the window.

I couldn't lie to her. "Not lately," I said.

"I want Harlan's photo back," she said.

Why couldn't I have just one picture of my daddy?

Why did she always have to have him for herself? That's how it had always been, her hogging what little he gave, even when he was gone.

"I don't know what you're talking about," I said. I could feel my nostrils flaring. We were quiet then. And after a while I asked, "Where did you get your snake bite scar?" She'd nearly died of it, she'd told Bee.

She looked at me, then turned back to the window. "What does it matter, Esme?"

It did mater, that we knew nothing of her, for the less we knew of her, the easier it was for her to slip away. Even though Bee had said that June Rain had nowhere to go, I knew she had a family somewhere, plus Harlan didn't have a destination either, and that didn't stop him. No sirree.

"I have something I want to show you," I told her. "It's about Harlan."

When June Rain followed me into the woods, the sun was starting to set, squatting heavily on a fringe of trees, and sending fiery ambered streaks across the sky. I looked back at her every now and then to make sure she was still there, worried she would drift away never to be seen again, a ghost of the forest.

I kept on walking, thinking of her singing sweetly to that baby piglet, and how she'd clung to Bo when he was a baby, and how she hadn't wanted me. But Paps had, when he was alive. He'd loved me, had rocked me, had called me his butter bean. Tears sprung in my eyes, and I swatted them away, not wanting June Rain to see me cry.

A few minutes later we came to the little cabin. She stopped a few feet away, as though she was scared. She looked at me funny, like she'd never seen me before. "What is this?" she finally asked.

I opened the door. I leaned against it, waiting for her, wanting her to hurt. Finally she stepped inside.

Her eyes grew big as she walked around the small space looking at each painting carefully, then moving on to the next. She seemed happy to be among his paintings again. I decided not to tell her about the night swimmer and the rainbow boots. Maybe I *had* dreamed them up. My eyes flitted over to the spot where I'd seen the sleeping bag, but it was gone. I didn't know what to make of that. Had Harlan been here, and then disappeared again? Had I dreamed up the sleeping bag, too?

June Rain stopped in front of the painting of me on the easel. From a distance it didn't look much different than any of Harlan's "ain't-no-picture" paintings. But it was me.

She left the cabin a few minutes later, her face averted, the painting of me clutched to her chest. I shut the door and ran after her.

"June Rain!" I called. "June Rain!" But she kept on marching through the woods and didn't wait for me.

The next day when I came down from digging on Solace Hill, I saw the Bee Wagon flying up our drive. It screeched to a halt when Bee spotted me. She rolled down the window and motioned for me to get in. Something was up. Her eyes were wild. She turned the Wagon around and hit the gas. She didn't ask what I'd been doing or where I'd been. Maybe she knew. I glanced back as the Wagon went through the gate to see June Rain drift from the woods, from the direction of Harlan's hut, the piglet clutched to her chest.

"All day I've felt something," Bee said as we roared down the road.

I put my seatbelt on and pulled it tight. I noticed a witching stick, holly perhaps, at my feet.

"I've been feeling like something is awfully wrong. Whatever it is, it's no good, Esme. Everything that's been going on, now something else is coming. I came home with Bo to the phone ringing off the hook. It was Miss Treva, doing her best to tell me something was wrong without everyone up and down our road hearing. She told me to get there quick. I could tell from her voice it's awful, something awful."

I didn't say a word as we flew down country roads, sometimes feeling like we were on two wheels around the bends, almost hitting a dog, and then barely missing a jackrabbit. I'd never seen my grandma so riled up. Never. This was ten times worse than the shotgun blast. My toes started to vibrate, a low tender hum that seemed to say, *Stay away.*

Finally we pulled into Miss Treva's drive. She was waiting for us on the front porch.

Bee got out of the Wagon, and I thought for a moment I should bring her witching stick, but then realized, as Bee must have, that she didn't need it. I followed her up the steps.

"Luther's missing again," Miss Treva said calmly, almost too calmly. But her face was as white as a ghost, her eyes stricken.

"You didn't call me all the way out here for that," Bee snapped.

I looked at her wondering why she was in such a tizzy. She'd said it was something big and awful. She was usually so calm, so calm, when she was called to find something.

"I heard a gunshot last night," Miss Treva said. She tilted her head toward the woods. "Out there. I was too scared to go see for myself and . . ." Her voice cracked. "And when he didn't come home, I knew something bad must've happened to him."

Bee turned and started for the woods, at first walking fast, then running. I followed her, but she yelled at me to stay back with Miss Treva. I ignored her. She ran on and I ran on after her into the woods, even though I couldn't feel my feet anymore. They were numb.

When we reached the clearing, Bee stopped. At first I only saw that dizzying swirl of pipes, tubes, and barrels—the moonshining equipment. A strange whistle sounded every few seconds as though the whole thing were on its last legs. I followed Bee's gaze. Someone was on the ground. Still. Motionless. Wearing Harlan's rainbow boots.

CHAPTER 12

A leaf fluttered from one of the trees, landing with a hushed *whoosh*, a fly droned, and the taste of honey from breakfast still on the roof of my mouth was sweet. My fingers and toes started to vibrate again, and I think I said aloud, "Yes, I know. I know. It's here. You can stop now. Leave me alone. Go away." The sky started to turn black, and I closed my eyes, picturing Harlan, smiling big at that gas pump, far away from us. "Why did you come back? Why did you come back?"

"It's not him." Bee's voice sounded muted, like it was coming through a scratchy transistor radio. I opened my eyes. I was kneeling on the ground. A scream pierced the air. I turned and saw Miss Treva ten yards behind me, clutching a tree.

"It's not Luther either," Bee called.

I got up off my knees. I gathered my courage and looked. It definitely wasn't Harlan. This man, whoever he was, was a good bit taller, and he had long brownish hair, sunk-in cheeks, and a long beard, like a hippie. I thought he kinda looked like Jesus. Jesus, lying next to barrels of moonshine with a rose tattoo on his arm. I knew it was disrespectful, but a wave of warm relief washed through me. My eyes traveled from his face to his chest where blood had seeped through his shirt, a perfect bull's-eye. I quickly looked away.

"He must've surprised the moonshiners," Bee said. "Go call Sheriff Finney," she yelled to Miss Treva.

"But Bee, Luther, the others . . . ," she screamed back.

Oh, God. My heart squeezed, thinking how Granger might be involved in all this and how much this was going to hurt Finch. This wasn't a little notch of Aberdeen sadness; this was a whopper.

"There ain't no way of getting around it, Treva," said Bee as she knelt down next to the man. "No

way we going to try to hide this. Go now!" When
Miss Treva didn't budge, Bee stood up and hollered. "In heaven's name go! A man's been killed
here." And finally Miss Treva turned and ran back
through the woods.

I inched forward, wanting to get a better look at
the boots. They were exactly the same, everything
was, even the pink splatter from when Harlan had
painted the Just Teasin' for Sweetmaw, and the yellow
splatter from painting the Galloways' front hallway.
Bee looked at the boots, too, then said softly, "I had a
vision . . . my boy's boots . . . I thought . . ." She knelt
down and reached into the man's pocket and pulled
out a wallet, seeming to know just where it would be.

"Who is he?" I asked.

She mumbled as she searched in a side com-
partment of the wallet. She held something up
and turned it over so I could see. It was a photo
of June Rain. She was young in the picture, very
young, smiling wistfully for the camera, her face
surrounded by tiny pinpricks of light, like fireflies.
She was wearing an odd, old-fashioned calico dress,
like something Laura Ingalls Wilder wore in *Little*

House on the Prairie, and her hair was in long black braids. The photo was well-worn like it had been looked at many times.

Bee turned it over. I leaned in and read "To Harlan, from June Rain." Bee stuffed it in her pocket. I wanted to look at the dead man's face again, see if there was any resemblance to any of us, but I was sick to my stomach now, thinking I might barf at any moment. I closed my eyes. *Uncle Hen.* It couldn't be. Something real from June Rain's past had wriggled up from the deep and found its way here.

"We don't know anything about him, which is the truth, Esme," Bee said flatly. Then she pulled a pack of Salems out of his other pocket and held them up. "Knowing that he was also smoking the same cigarettes as Harlan is not going to help anyone in any way."

"But why does he have a picture of June Rain?" I asked.

"Don't know. Don't want to know," Bee said gruffly as she stood up and brushed the dirt off her dungarees.

The sound of sirens pierced the woods. If Harlan wasn't wearing his own boots, maybe he wasn't alive either. Maybe he was also somewhere in these trees with a seeping red bull's-eye across *his* chest. My stomach turned and the world began to blacken, till I felt Bee's hand on my back, holding me up, keeping me from falling again.

"There, there," she said. "It's not Harlan."

She sat me down on a log and told me to breathe.

When Sheriff Finney reached us, he told Bee to take me on home and scolded her for bringing me here in the first place, letting me see a dead body, and getting involved in police business. He said he'd come over and ask her questions later.

Bee got Miss Treva into bed, Miss Treva mumbling "But Luther, where is he?" *And where's Granger?* I thought to myself. *And Harlan?* Then Bee drove us home in the Bee Wagon as I tried to quiet my spinning mind. What if Bee had told the sheriff about the moonshine when we'd first found it? Would that man still be alive? What if I'd told Bee about seeing the night swimmer, the rainbow boots, Harlan's cabin, the sleeping bag? Would that have changed a thing?

When we pulled up the drive, Sugar Pie was roaming between the peach trees and Bo was trying to catch her. And I thought about *him*, that dead man, who might have been the one standing there in the darkness, smoking Harlan's cigarettes, watching our house. Watching us. Watching June Rain. Shivers crept up my back. *Was he Uncle Hen?* Why was he wearing my daddy's boots? Had he hurt Harlan in some way?

June Rain was on the kitchen steps, the piglet in her arms. Sweetmaw was there, too, looking worried. Old Jack peered through the screen door looking like someone had swatted him on the head. I didn't think he liked that piglet one bit.

Bee brushed past everyone and went inside, and I ran to the orchard to help Bo.

"June Rain thinks Harlan's coming home," he said.

"No," I said as I grabbed Sugar Pie's halter from him. "No, he's not coming home." I didn't want to say it, that he was never coming home; I couldn't do that to Bo. But I didn't think he was. Someone else had come, come with Harlan's rainbow boots on.

I hid under the house when Sheriff Finney pulled up a couple of hours later and hauled his fat self out of his squad car. He told Bee he was arresting her for not reporting what she knew about the illegal moonshining and that if she'd done so, none of this would have happened. She was an accessory to a murder, or something like that. I peered out between the wooden slats when he pulled away a few minutes later with Bee inside the car.

It was hot that night, and I lay on the quilt under the tractor waiting for Finch, hoping one minute that he'd come, the next that he wouldn't. He must have heard the news by now. After the sheriff had taken Bee away, we'd sat around the table in silence, June Rain petting Jewell, Bo still sniffling, while the phone rang again and again.

It was deathly quiet on Solace Hill except for the low buzzing of June bugs around the lantern. The crickets were silent, as though they were listening. Bump was next to me on the quilt. I lay there thinking about Paps and how I wasn't so sure I felt him with me anymore when I ran my fingers through the earth.

I heard someone coming up the hill. A moment later Finch stuck his head under the tractor.

"Did you know, Esme?" he asked.

There were lots of things he could be referring to, but I knew he was talking about Granger.

"Yes," I said. "I was with Bee when we found the moonshine. Granger was there with Luther Stump and Johnny Wallet. I didn't want to hurt you, Finch. That's why I didn't tell you."

"You knew when I was wearing those stupid moon boots and new jeans and eating Bottle Caps and Red Hots and . . ." His eyes grew wide remembering. "You even ate some and you knew! You're supposed to be my best friend and you didn't even tell me."

Bump ran out from under the tractor, startling Finch.

"Holy Mary, what in the heck was that?" he yelled.

"Bump," I said, crawling out. I sat down next to

Louella Goodbones. I put my hand on top of her head and breathed in deep and hard.

"Who was the dead man?" Finch asked a moment later. He was still standing there gawking at me like he'd never seen me before.

"I don't know," I said, and that was the truth. "But I think he might've known Harlan and maybe June Rain, too."

Finch finally sat down next to me and went to work digging around Louella Goodbones. The very tippy-top of her backbone was starting to show. She was emerging from her hillside grave. But did I really want her to? Did she want to?

"Bee's in jail," I said.

Finch didn't say anything, just kept on clearing the dirt.

"Sweetmaw says Sheriff Finney doesn't have a good reason to hold her. Says we should be able to get her out, maybe tomorrow. Sweetmaw's staying here to take care of us. She closed up the shop early today. She's cooking up a storm. I don't think she's ever stayed with us, ever. . . ." I trailed off when Finch looked at me and frowned. He pushed his glasses up and continued to dig.

"June Rain's named that piglet Jewell." I snorted. "She's still treating it like a real baby."

"Are you ready yet?" he asked, looking up at me, the lantern illuminating his face.

Butterflies fluttered in my stomach then, seeing him like that, looking like the boys on the magazines that Rose Galloway and Mady Whitshaw always pawed through, even if he did have a cowlick and glasses. A new Finch was underneath, waiting to come out. I wasn't sure I wanted that. I was never going to emerge from my Thumbelina stage, ever. I'd always be that tiny butter bean.

"For what?" I asked.

"For showing the world what you have here," he said, gesturing to the bones.

"No," I said. "Not yet."

An hour later Finch left. Then Old Jack was barking and there he was with Bo.

"Sweetmaw's worried about you," Bo told me. "She wants to know where you are."

I realized how nice that was, that someone was worried about me.

"June Rain took that pig with her up to her room again," he said.

"I know, Bo," I said, rubbing his head.

I followed him back down the hill and into the kitchen. Sweetmaw had filled every counter with all sorts of baked goods and casseroles. She turned to me, her arms wide. She folded me up in them and I never wanted to let go. No one had held me like that since Paps.

CHAPTER 13

I lay in bed listening to the hushed voices down in the kitchen. Sweetmaw and June Rain were talking about Bee and what they were going to do. Bo was sleeping next to me, twitching every now and then, and I envied his sweetness and ignorance. Old Jack was in the bed, too, warm at my feet.

I crept downstairs and hid behind the kitchen doorway. The piglet was crying again. I didn't know a pig could squeal so much.

"Here, hand her to me," Sweetmaw demanded. "Poor thing."

It was quiet as June Rain gave Jewell to Sweetmaw, but then she started crying out again like someone was poking her with a needle.

"Here, have her back," Sweetmaw said.

June Rain started humming and Jewell quieted down.

"So we need a hundred fifty dollars to get Bee out of jail," Sweetmaw said. "I can help a little but not a whole lot. You sure Bee don't have any cash stowed away here?"

"Pretty sure," June Rain said.

"Well, we're in a right pickle," Sweetmaw said. "As much as I want to leave Bee McCauley in the slammer a good long while to teach her a lesson, we *can't* leave her in there. Both of us need to be at the Just Teasin' today; there's a country club luncheon and all the ladies are coming in. Esme and Bo are too young to be here all day by themselves."

"They'd be okay," said June Rain.

It was true we'd be okay; we always were. But her words still stung, as they almost always did when she chose to speak, as much for what she said as for what she didn't.

"True-itt," said Sweetmaw, and I had to think a minute before realizing she was talking about Sheriff Finney, "said the dead man's name was Wilson Henry."

I peeked around the door to see June Rain's reaction, thinking about the photograph of her in that strange prairie dress, her hair long and curly, those funny points of light around her head. Bee'd said June Rain had buried everything deep, so deep you'd need a polecat to pull it all out. She'd turned her head suddenly, looking out the kitchen window. I could just see the gentle profile of her face, her mouth slightly open, a slow blink.

"He was fifty-five or so, True-itt said," Sweetmaw continued. "Maybe older. Hard to tell under all that hippie hair. Not sure where he's actually from. He went under many aliases, it appears. Might've been a traveling man, a hobo, True-itt thinks, who stumbled on Luther's business by accident. True-itt's trying to find his kin.

"Poor Pearl Mae," Sweetmaw continued. "I remember when Granger was knee-high to a grasshopper. Cute as a bug, for an Aberdeen. That Finch's gonna turn out okay, hopefully. One can't help who your kin is; you're stuck with them. Has Bee harvested the honey yet? How much money did that bring in?"

"Yes, she and Esme did," said June Rain, turning back to Sweetmaw, her face devoid of anything might have been there a moment before. "But she didn't sell it all yet. It would take us another week, driving all around the county."

"What's she doing making Esme help with the bees? As I recall, that child had a deathly fear of them since she was a little one."

"Bee says it comes natural to Esme," said June Rain.

Ha. *Natural.*

"You all seem to think everything comes natural to that poor little thing. She's only a child. Seems tough, but she's not. That little heart of hers is as tender as they come."

"She's twelve," said June Rain, "almost thirteen. I'd seen more by her age than anyone can imagine."

My ears perked up. I'd never ever heard June Rain talk about her childhood, not once. Did I imagine a light edge in her voice? Surely Sweetmaw, the queen of all gossips, would nose out more. But to my surprise, she let it go and went back to talking about Bee's bail money.

I wondered how much the gold coin in the bee box up on Solace Hill was worth. Would it be enough to bail Bee out? Surely a solid gold coin had to be enough.

I walked into the kitchen. "I can get the money," I said.

Sweetmaw's mouth dropped open and her eyes narrowed. June Rain turned her face away, and that stung as though one of Bee's bees had landed on my heart.

I raced out of the house, screen door slamming, and ran up Solace Hill, to the tractor, to Louella Goodbones. Fireflies flew around me, blinking and blinking, as though trying to tell me something. *No. No. Leave it there!* And then they slowly flew down the hill in formation before suddenly disappearing. My toes started to tingle, almost like a burn and I ran back down the hill, where Sweetmaw and Old Jack met me.

"Violet Galloway just called. Said she was posting the bail. Said something about you finding a popsicle."

* * *

The next morning June Rain stayed home with Bo while I rode with Sweetmaw in the Buick to get Bee out of jail. Old Jack rode in the backseat, with his head out the window.

"Why didn't you ask June Rain what she saw when she was twelve?" I said as we drove past the Aberdeens'. Sweetmaw drove as slow as a turtle, the opposite of Bee in her wagon.

"I don't bother to ask a question for answers I'm not going to get in a million years, Esme," she said. "Maybe you should ask her. Maybe she'll tell you. But for right now, she doesn't want anyone to find out, and perhaps that's just how it should stay. You gotta know when to leave something alone. That was always Bee's problem, not leaving things be."

A car full of teenagers zoomed past, honking as it sped in front of us. I sunk down low in my seat.

"I've been finding things," I whispered to myself.

Sweetmaw looked over at me quickly with worried eyes. "Oh, no," she said, stepping on the gas. Then she shook her head, as though changing her mind, and pulled the car off the road.

It was quiet except for the sound of Old Jack panting. "Our grandmother May could foresee the future," Sweetmaw said. "And our mother the weather. And then one day, Bee. But Bee was different. More powerful, a force of nature." She paused and I stared at the cornfield next to us, watching the breeze lift the hat off an old scarecrow.

"Did anything ever happen to Bee before her gift came to her?" I asked her.

"Whatever do you mean?'

"Like lightning, or a storm?"

Sweetmaw looked at me strangely like I'd asked the stupidest question on earth. "Why yes, honey," she said. "Bee was a baby, just a little thing. I was playing on the front porch when a tornado come barreling toward the house; I barely made it in under a table. The house was directly hit, most of the roof torn off. I found Mama in a doorway, her head hit mighty hard, and Bee sleeping peacefully in her bassinet. Bee had slept through it all untouched.

"Then when I was ten, Bee about eight, I'd been playing with Mama's china teapot out in the back pasture, having a mud tea party. I'd broken it, buried it right there down deep. I was the naughty one, back then, if you can believe it. Bee was the prized child, the smart one, the beautiful one. And we didn't get along.

"Mama fussed up quite a storm when she discovered her teapot was missing. Then Bee, who was already sewing those quilts, got a funny look on her face like she'd bitten down on a bug. She marched out to the pasture, dug it straight up, marched back in, and handed the pieces to Mama. I got a whuppin'. And that's how it started, right out of nowhere. Secretly, I used to hate her for it, all the things she found. Some things better left buried." Sweetmaw paused. "But maybe it did start with that tornado. I never thought of that. Fittin', for Bee is like a tornado." Old Jack leaned his head between us as though he were listening in, too.

"All the attention she got, admiration, little gifts," Sweetmaw continued. "She was even written up in the paper with a photo." She chuckled. "Had found Old Man Finney's World War One medals buried in his backyard." She wiggled her hand in the air in a lah-di-dah gesture.

"Then I realized that what Bee had was a burden and maybe *I* was the lucky one. And it was quite the revelation. Sweetmaw Hennessey was the lucky one. Can you imagine that? Even if she was a little bit prettier," and here she looked over at me, her eyes twinkling. "And smarter. Even if she got a good husband and I never had one. She was going to have a harder time in life, always stirred up. I think I knew that deep down even when we were kids."

I could always count on Sweetmaw to tell the truth. Old Jack licked me up the side of the face. He was licking away a tear that I didn't know had fallen.

"Did anything happen when Harlan was a baby?" I asked.

Sweetmaw frowned. "Do you mean if Bee dropped that rascal on his head or something?" She snorted. "If you're asking if he was born that way, always leaving you, honey, I don't think so. But Bee and I didn't talk for many years, so I don't know."

I looked out the window a moment. "At least he's never hurt anyone, though," I whispered.

"That's not good enough, honey," Sweetmaw

said. "Being harmless. Doesn't make him a decent human being. I'm gonna tear off a strip of him next time he comes home."

If he does, I thought.

"Bee says it's a gift from God," I said a little while later. "The gift of finding things."

"It may be, Esme." She reached over, pulling my chin toward her. "Or it just might be about growing up and noticing what's around you, honey, what you can fix and what you can't. What people are about, what they want, what they wish for, their hopes and their dreams. Pretend it's a present, wrapped, that you can put away till you're grown up and ready."

But it had already been opened, whatever it was. My feet started to vibrate then, and I knew with certainty that something was buried next to us in the cornfield, a cowbell of some sort with a heart engraved on it that had meant all the world to someone at some time. Sweetmaw started up the pink Buick again, and we drove on down the road, that vibrating, lawn mower feeling moving up my legs as the tears rolled down my face.

* * *

We pulled up to the jail and Sweetmaw left Old Jack and me in the car while she went in for Bee. I slid down in my seat hoping no one could see me, but it was boiling hot already and I had to roll down the window. I stretched out, suddenly feeling tired. Old Jack lay down on the backseat and started to snore.

I don't know how much later it was, but I realized the sun was no longer shining on me. I opened an eye and saw someone standing by my window. I bolted up.

It was Finch's mama. She had her church coat on, one side of her hairdo teased up a little higher than the other. She must've just come out of the jailhouse and had wanted to look presentable for Sheriff Finney.

"Have they found Granger yet?" I asked her, not wanting to know, not really. I couldn't meet her eyes.

She shook her head and bit her lip just like Finch does.

She looked around. Bee had told me that Pearl Mae was pretty once and had been voted "Most

Likely to Go to College" in her class at Hollis High and had won state for twirling, but somehow she'd ended up with Spoon. He was handsome, Bee explained, and that's sometimes enough to bring a pretty girl down.

Finally Pearl Mae found her words. "Does Bee have any sense of where Granger is?" she asked.

"I don't think so, Mrs. Aberdeen," I said. "I'm sorry," I said a moment later, afraid to look at her, afraid she might know it all, how I maybe could've kept her son from getting into the big trouble he was in now. She looked like she was going to say something, but she didn't, and I wondered how it was even possible that she was once a beautiful girl who could throw a twirling baton into the air and catch it. Then she left and I leaned back into the seat, wishing I could disappear, too.

"I heard about Bee," said a soft voice. Mady Whitshaw was standing next to the car.

"Is that so?" I asked. "Well, what else do you have to say to me?"

"Just that I'm sorry. For everything. Not just

school. I'm sorry."

I couldn't look at her.

Finally she added, "My mama hurts all the time, Esme. All the time. That's all I wanted to say."

Sweetmaw drove us back to Peach Hollow Farm while Bee fumed. I think I could almost see steam coming out of her ears. I sat in the backseat with Old Jack's head in my lap, hoping she'd forget about me.

"Where'd you get the money?" she said to no one in particular. Old Jack smelled something out the window and scrambled off of me. Bee caught my eye in the rearview mirror. "You didn't find anything up on that hill, did you, Esme?"

I didn't answer and looked away.

"You should've just let me stay in there. The sheriff knew he had no basis for keeping me. Would've let me out eventually." She eyed me again, looking at me funny.

"*Mmm-hmmm,*" said Sweetmaw. "True-itt said he's tired of you taking the law into your own hands, Bee. I don't think he'll let this one go. There's a dead man lying in the morgue over in Paradise and no one knows who he is."

I stared out the window. Wilson Henry. Wilson *Hen*-ry.

"True-itt, huh?" Bee said, one eyebrow raised. "Aren't you too old for romance?"

Sweetmaw ignored her. "True-itt says he hasn't forgotten the time you found that gun off Highway Ten, the one that had been used in a holdup in Dallas. If you'd turned it in sooner, they might have caught those no-good thieves."

Bee shook her head. "I needed it to get rid of the squirrels," she snapped. "They were eating my peaches."

"Some things don't ever change," said Sweetmaw.

"Nope, sure they don't," said Bee.

I knew there was a lot more to their words, lots of broken pieces that might never be mended.

That night Bo came into my room with his baby blanket, somehow resurrected from somewhere. We'd had a reheated dinner of baked beans and cornbread. June Rain had gone to her room with

Jewell after we'd finished and had shut the door. Bo was sucking his thumb, something he hadn't done since Bee'd put honey mixed with Tabasco on it when he was three.

"The dead man's not Daddy?" he whispered.

I moved over and patted the spot next to me. "No," I said. "Don't worry. It's not Harlan."

Our daddy was still out there, still alive, wandering, probably bootless, but still wandering like he always had. When I was younger, I'd asked Bee why if she could find anything in the world, she couldn't find Harlan. I knew now that perhaps you can't find the things that are the most precious to you.

"Can that dinosaur come live with us?" Bo said as he climbed under the chenille with me.

"No." I sighed. "She's too big, Bo, way too big."

He snuggled under my arm, then looked up at me, his eyes full of worry. "Where do fireflies go to die?" he said. "Is there a heaven for them?"

"Of course, Bo," I answered. "Of course."

I'd wondered the same thing since Bee had said they were disappearing. Where *did* they go? To be with the ghosts of this world? I pulled Bo closer, snuggling till he finally fell asleep. I kissed his forehead, smelling the little boyness of him. I thought of Louella Goodbones on Solace Hill coming up from the earth. And I thought of bootless Harlan out there and how little he knew of us.

CHAPTER 14

There are things we know for sure and things we don't. It's the unknown, the unexpected, the tornado that turns on you in a moment that are the most troubling. And there's nothing you can do about it but wait. A week had gone by and there was still no sign of Granger, Luther, or Johnny. Finch told me his daddy had spent days driving all over the county looking for Granger but came home hollow eyed. Spoon'd thrown all of Granger's new clothes on the trash heap.

Sheriff Finney told Sweetmaw that the dead man had been killed by a blast from a shotgun at close range. He'd searched the Stump house for a shotgun but didn't find one. And that dead man was still over in the Paradise morgue because no kin came forward and the sheriff still wasn't sure who he really was.

I'd been waiting, wondering if Bee was going to turn over the photo of June Rain, like she'd eventually turned over the squirrel-shooting gun. Turn over that wallet, too, she'd taken from his pants. But I had a feeling she wouldn't. Not this time. Especially not that mystery photo. It was from the sweet far in-between, and there was no telling what it let loose upon us.

Jewell still squealed, and now Old Jack howled like a wolf when she did. So Bee finally said enough is enough and a piglet needs fresh air and she made a little enclosure for Jewell in the shade of the peach orchard. Now Jewell ran around happily with a little bell on a velvet choker in case she got out. June Rain was allowed to bring her inside for an hour a day, and Bo had started taking her on walks.

June Rain changed when Jewell was moved outside, and I think she'd now given up on hoping that Harlan was coming home. I'd heard her footsteps in the night, pausing by my door, then going downstairs, and a moment later the gentle slap of the screen door. I knew where she went and didn't feel bad that I'd showed her the cabin. We all need something to hang on to.

Finch and I worked every night up on Solace Hill, uncovering more and more of Louella Goodbones. He asked me every night if I was ready to show her to the world, and every night I'd say no. Louella Goodbones was going to stay here. Strangely, I'd felt less and less of Paps the more we dug away at her, and I hated that I didn't know where he was anymore. Maybe he was on his way to heaven, following the fireflies.

One morning when I woke up, cocooned under my chenille blanket, I had a feeling that something wasn't right over at Miss Lilah's. Finch and I had not been to see her in a while. Maybe that's all it was.

But I couldn't let it be. A little bit later, when I walked up her steps, Miss Opal met me at the door. "She's had a minor stroke in the night, Esme. Said she saw a ghost." Shivers went up my back as she continued. "Doc Delaney wanted to take her to the hospital in Paradise, but she refused. Says it's her time to go."

I turned to leave, saying I was sorry.

"No, no. Please come see her," Miss Opal said. "She's been asking for you all morning. Says she has something to tell you. She keeps insisting the Lord is calling her home. Says she wants to be buried in her best dress, with her pearls, too. Says if she's going to meet her maker, she better be dressed right." She led me to a back bedroom.

I followed her, afraid of what I might see. But it was just Miss Lilah.

"It's my time, Esme," she said when she saw me, her voice raspy, her face twisted-up funny. "You know it was your Grandpa Homer I saw law night." Shivers went up my spine, all the way up till my ears tingled.

"Now why would he be coming to see you?" I asked, and she laughed.

"Got the Hennessey sass, I see. I didn't think you had it in you. Thought you had more of the McCauley quiet, like Homer." Her eyes shut.

"Miss Lilah," I said. Her eyes fluttered open.

"Oh, yes," she said. "Where were we? Homer. He appeared at my bedside in the middle of the night, said he was on his way to heaven and would I like to catch a ride. Standing there sure as daylight in his church suit. Said he'd be back for me in just a bit; he had some unfinished business."

Jealousy shot through me. All that time I'd been up on the hill. Why hadn't he talked to me? "But why you, Miss Lilah?"

"I'm the oldest in all of Hollis; guess my ticket is expired." She laughed.

"Did he say anything else?" I asked.

"Said to tell you to bring her up and let her go."

Shivers went down my arms. Was she talking about Louella Goodbones?

"And to forgive Bee for what she'd done for Harlan. He'd forgiven her and understood it all, now that he was in-between."

What had Bee done for Harlan?

"Does this have anything to do with the ghost lights you saw, way back when Harlan was a baby, going up and down Solace Hill?"

She didn't answer. She closed her eyes and fell asleep. I lingered there a long time, watching her chest go up and down before quietly slipping out.

* * *

I rode my bike home, the gentle rain misting my face, thinking how some people say a rain means a stranger is coming. I thought about Jewell arriving, and then that dead man, and wondered who was coming next. I lifted my face up to the sky, opening my mouth to catch what I could, relishing the sweetness of it. I thought about Paps, and how he barely said a word to me but I knew he loved me just the same. I'd always been quiet, too, holding all those worries in, but I felt different now. A new me was opening up. I wasn't sure what it all meant.

I was hoping I could go straight up to Solace Hill, but just my luck, Bee was picking peaches. Jewell wasn't in her enclosure; June Rain must have brought her in. I slowed down, hoping I could bike across the front lawn without Bee seeing me. She called me over without even looking up.

"Where you been?" she asked after I leaned my bike against a tree.

"Visiting Miss Lilah," I said. "She had a stroke last night. Thinks she's going to die."

She glanced over at me, then went back to picking. "That lady's old, Esme. Maybe it's her time."

"Doc Delaney says she should be taken to the hospital."

She yanked at a peach that wasn't quite ready. Bee'd been out of sorts, more than usual, since that banker Mr. Galloway had attempted a second visit and being put in jail. "Life is unpredictable, Esme. It's always ready to bite you in the butt when you least expect it."

"Are there ghosts, Bee?" I asked her. "Do ghosts come along with our gift?"

She pursed her lips, yanking on another unripe peach. "Why you ask, honey?"

Suddenly a jackrabbit shot by with Old Jack right on its tail. It escaped under the pasture fence, where Sugar Pie was grazing.

"Miss Lilah said she saw Paps. In his church suit."

Bee clasped the peach hard, looking at me.

Finally she said, "He was wearing that suit the day we got married, only time I ever got him in a suit, got him in a church."

"Do ghosts come with our gift, Bee?" I asked again.

She leaned her head against the tree. "I was

hoping you wouldn't get one," she said softly. "None of the others before us, none of our grandmothers did. I've been so worried for you, Esme. . . . "

"It's all right, Bee," I said, glancing over at the henhouse, then up to Solace Hill. "I think mine just came to show me something, to help me, then it went away."

She looked over at me, her eyes glistening with relief. "They don't always go easily."

"Bee, what happened when Harlan . . ."

"You go on in out of the rain, Esme," she said quietly, her head still resting on the trunk of the peach tree.

I waited a minute for her to say something more but she didn't.

When I reached the screen door, I didn't go in right away. I watched June Rain, Jewell in one arm, the other wrapped around Bo, who was leaning in to his mama as far as he could. June Rain was humming and it took me a second to realize it was another church hymn: "I go by the wayside, I go by the wayside." I listened in wonder, knowing this would have to go under the revival tent, with Uncle Hen and the bubblegum snakebite scar and all the other things we didn't know about her. Finally I turned and ran for Solace Hill even though the rain was coming down harder now, unleashed from the sky.

I curled up on Bee's quilt under the tractor. Bump was nearby munching on a worm. *Paps, where are you?* I was the one who'd loved him the most, who missed him more than anything in the world. Why hadn't he come for me, then? I watched the rain as it washed down on Louella Goodbones, revealing more and more of her. It was the rain that had shown her to me in the first place. No, it was Paps, it was Paps who'd led me to her. Or had it started before?

One small thing could lead to another. The ripple effect. Had it started with the lightning the day Paps died? Or when I followed the fireflies up the hill? Or were the answers floating around in the sweet far in-between? Bee said there were vibes out there, and that she and I just picked up more than others did, as though we had antennae. Maybe this hill put off a whole mess of signals, maybe it had since that dinosaur lay down and died millions of years ago.

Bring her up and let her go.

But I wasn't ready. She was all I had. Maybe it was true that our sorrows were interlinked like the honeycombs, one after the other like Bee said. But I had to believe that somehow, some way, eventually a joy would follow. I'd already helped people like Dovie, and Rose, and maybe I could do more.

And then I heard a voice. It sounded strange and sad, and so, so far away like a ship's foghorn calling to its port. I was imagining it, wasn't I?

I crawled out from under the tractor, muddying my knees and hands. I slipped as I tried to stand up, and slid down the hill a little bit. Through the rain I could see a tall figure—a man— and a child next to him. *Paps?*

"Here I am!" I called, waving my hands in the rain, squinting to keep the water out of my eyes.

"Esme?" It was Bo next to the man, waving at me excitedly.

He was a tall man dressed in khaki wearing a safari hat. *A safari hat.* Something tiny and small crawled across my heart then, and I couldn't breathe. He wore a special belt with brushes and picks dangling from it.

I stood there blinking, staring at that belt, knowing I'd somehow unleashed something, and that belt and that man were here because of me. I looked at Bo.

"Bee said he could find you up on the hill," he said, smiling big. "He's a dinosaur man," Bo said. "T-R-E-X."

The man smiled and reached out his hand to shake mine, but my legs were trembling and I couldn't move. Then I slowly pulled my hands behind my back, maybe hoping that by not taking his extended hand he would go away.

"Esme McCauley, you sent me a letter," he said. His voice had a strange light accent to it.

My heart fell to my feet. I had not sent the letter. Finch had done this, I knew it. My best friend in the world had done this. I looked back up the hill toward the tractor that thankfully blocked the view of what we'd uncovered. "I'm sorry Louella Goodbones," I whispered. "I'm so sorry."

CHAPTER 15

The man pushed his hat back slightly. He had long sandy brown hair that was tucked behind his ears, and his face was tanned, almost leathery. He was handsome in a strange sort of way.

I could see Bee in the distance, under the peach trees, holding an umbrella. I could hear Old Jack barking at the screen door, and somehow I knew that June Rain was standing at the window with Jewell.

The man pulled something from his back pocket. He unfolded it and held it out to me. I stared down at Finch's drawing of Louella Goodbones. It looked like it had been taken straight from a science book except for the cartoony eyes I'd drawn, which Finch had gussied up. My stomach dropped. I couldn't believe it. Couldn't believe it. *All* that time he'd been asking me if I was ready to send the letter and he'd already done it.

"I'm Professor Abramanov and I teach paleontology in Dallas," the man said. "I received this letter from an Esme McCauley and it very much intrigued me. So much so, I got in my car and drove to Hollis. Inquired about you at the library. Miss Ferriday gave me directions to your farm."

"What's paleon—" asked Bo

"He's a paleontologist," I said. "He's interested in my dinosaur."

"If you please, Miss McCauley, I'd like to know where you've seen *this*." He nodded at Finch's drawing. He was someone who didn't seem to practice the niceties of small talk, not like everyone in Hollis who danced like chickens around everything.

"Why?" I asked.

"Because I've never in all my years seen a skull like this. It's similar to a sauropod but not quite. The eye sockets are more rounded, and the snout more elongated. The eyes, well, they look pretty silly." He laughed. "Did you make this up? Please tell me you didn't."

I couldn't lie. He'd driven all the way out here. Bo knew, and Miss Ferriday might have let something slip when he'd gone by the library, and of course Finch had given everything away. My secret was no longer mine. "No, I didn't make it up. She's up there, up on the hill."

Bo let go of the man's hand and ran through the mud up Solace Hill.

"It's a *she*, is it?" the professor asked, chuckling. "Are you sure?"

"Sure as daylight," I said. I was soaked now, my toes squishy in my moccasins.

"We'll see about that. How did you find her?" he asked.

"Paps found her for me," I whispered.

"Can I see her?" But he was already following Bo up the hill, slipping a little in the mud, his tools clinking like wind chimes. Finally I snapped out of my daze and ran after him.

Professor Abramanov arrived at the top of the hill a few minutes after I had. I took a step back so he could see Louella Goodbones, and just as I did the sun peeked out, shining an arc of light on her skeleton. The professor stepped forward and his mouth dropped open and his eyes grew wide. He knelt down on one knee and ran his fingers across her snout, up and up and across her head. Then he gingerly brushed off her shoulder blade. He stood up and stepped back and stood there looking like I'd first seen him in that grainy photograph. Maybe I'd known even then that he would come, that Louella would pull him here. Maybe I'd known all along. He wiped his hand across his forehead like he'd just won a marathon.

"Well, what is she?" I asked. "Who is she?"

The professor shook his head. "I don't know," he said. "I just don't know. But that's a good thing, Miss McCauley. That's a very good thing."

Later we sat with the professor around the dinner table, all of us, including Sweetmaw and Jewell, her little bell tinkling as June Rain shifted her from one shoulder to another. Bee had made chicken-in-a-blanket with cornmeal dumplings, and hot rolls, and string beans with baby onions from her garden and chocolate nut angel pie. She'd even brought out Grandmother Hennessey's gold-rimmed china which we normally only used on Thanksgiving and Christmas. She kept pouring the professor more sweet tea and serving him second helpings.

"I haven't had a home-cooked meal like this in years," the professor said.

June Rain sat across the table from him, feeding Jewell with a bottle.

"Why do they call you T. Rex? 'Cause you found one?" asked Bo excitedly.

Professor Abramanov wiped his mouth with his napkin and shook his head. "No, can't say that I ever have, young man. My students nicknamed me T. Rex because my name is so hard to pronounce. They call me 'Professor T.' for short. You can call me that; it's easier for everyone."

"Where did you say you're from, Professor T.?" Sweetmaw asked with a giggle, her cheeks pink. She handed him the rolls at the same time Bee was handing him the chicken.

"Dallas, at Southern Methodist University, although I'm in the field half the year. It's usually just beans and franks and hard biscuits when I'm out working." He hadn't answered her question, not really. It was obvious he was originally from somewhere other than Texas even if he was nicknamed T. Rex.

Bee narrowed her eyes at him.

"And what is your specialty, Professor Abramanov?" Bee asked, not one for silly nicknames even if she had one herself.

Despite the worried feeling in my stomach, I couldn't help chomping down on the cornmeal dumplings, my favorite.

"Carnivores from the late Cretaceous period," he replied, then added, "That's around sixty-five million years ago."

"There's a whole lot of years gone by since then, Professor T.," Sweetmaw said.

June Rain shifted Jewell, who was sleeping, to her other shoulder, and I noticed that the piglet was wearing little lace bloomers that someone had embroidered *Jewell* on, which I thought was the strangest thing since I'd never seen a needle in June Rain's hands before. The professor was looking at June Rain while he went on telling us about his work and using a whole bunch of big words none of us had ever heard of and would forget in five minutes. I glanced over at Bee, and she was holding the bowl of string beans in midair, her eyes narrowed on the professor.

"So just what has Esme found up on that hill?" she interrupted him, getting right to the point. "What is it that made you get in your car and drive all the way from some college in Dallas?"

"Southern Methodist University," he said, smiling slightly as he sipped his sweet tea.

"I heard you before," said Bee gruffly. "Don't matter where you're *from*, just want to know why you're *here*. And what you want from us."

"Why is Bee mad?" Bo whispered to me.

It was quiet a moment, then Professor T. said, "Mrs. McCauley, I don't know what Esme found. It's a dinosaur, that's for sure, and it's a genus I've never seen before. I don't think that anyone has ever seen it before. I think perhaps it might be a theropod because the snout resembles an Allosaurus, but more elongated — and it's smaller than an Allosaurus and other theropods. The conical teeth have trailing edge serrations, which is what a carnivore needs to crush bones, and from what I can see of the shoulder musculature, it had bipedal posture."

Sweetmaw was giggling again, her face pinked all the way to her ears. "My, my Professor T., you sure know how to use big words!" She tried to take Jewell from June Rain then, but Jewell snorted so Sweetmaw bit into her roll with an offended look instead.

"That dinosaur is on our property, Professor," said Bee. "Get to it. Just what do you want from us?"

"Mrs. McCauley," he said. "I like you."

"Well, I don't think I like you," Bee said.

"Don't mind her," Sweetmaw said. "She's a little hard around the edges, Professor, that's all."

"I deal with all kinds of people in my work," said Professor T. "I can handle myself." But he wasn't smiling anymore.

Bee scooted away from the table, her chair screeching across the linoleum. Everyone watched her as she went to peer out the screen door, then just stood there, her arms folded across her chest. Old Jack trotted over and sat down behind her, thumping his tail. A slight breeze wafted in, and I thought

I could smell Harlan's cigarettes. Bee just looked out into the darkness, waiting for the professor to tell her what he wanted. Suddenly two fireflies landed on the screen door, their embering tails blinking. The hairs stood up on my neck.

"I want it, Mrs. McCauley. Whatever it is up there. I want it more than anything in the world. Something like this only comes along once in a lifetime for someone like me." He paused, and I could see he was measuring his words, thinking it all through. "I have no doubt my department, the university even, will be willing to pay you for it."

Bee stood there, her back to us. I started to feel dizzy when Old Jack got up and wagged his tail, sniffing at the fireflies on the screen.

"Once in a lifetime," Bee mumbled. "Once in a lifetime." She paused, then added, "Well, in that case, other people are going to want it, too, aren't they, Professor?"

Professor T. was smiling like a lizard. I have to admit, it made him really handsome. Really, really handsome. Movie-star handsome.

But I could see a glimmer of fear in his eyes, too,

fear that his dream was about to be snatched away from him. "I hope we don't have to come to that. I have to talk to the higher-ups, there will have to be meetings, decisions made. But whatever we offer, it will be fair. I promise you that, Mrs. McCauley. It will be fair and I will take care of her and eventually she will be shared with the world."

Bee snorted. "*Her.* You sure it's a her, Professor?"

"Esme McCauley thinks so, and I believe her." He winked at me and I looked away.

"But no one has asked me," I whispered. "I found her. Maybe she wants to stay right where she is."

Everyone looked at me. The money from selling Louella Goodbones would save the farm. That's what Bee wanted. And that's what Paps would want. Perhaps that's why he'd led me up there in the first place.

Bee looked at me, her eyes questioning. She was leaving it all up to me, and I shook my head at her. Tears began to prick at my eyes. I didn't want to lose her, my Louella Goodbones.

"All right," I whispered, then louder. "All right!" I pushed away from the table, knocking my chair over. I ran past Bee, letting the door slam in her face. I ran as fast as I could through the dark, my feet on fire, the smell of Harlan's Salems tickling my nose. I glanced back and saw the fireflies trailing behind me like tiny stars.

I sat under the peach trees for a good long time. Watching the goings-on in the kitchen, shadows walking to and fro as dishes were done and put away, listening to the low mumblings of conversations as decisions were made, my stomach growling when I realized I'd missed out on the chocolate nut angel pie. Then the lights went off one by one as everyone prepared for bed, and Sweetmaw drove down the drive. Professor T. never came out, so I figured Bee had invited him to stay the night. Bee'd have to put him in Paps's room; there was no place else. I didn't like that idea one bit.

This was all Finch's doing. My heart hurt thinking about it. I didn't know if it would ever feel the same up on Solace Hill for me. A profound sadness washed through me like a warm wave.

I got up and ran off into the darkness, not slowing

down till I reached Finch's house. I crept around to the back, tripping and falling flat on my face in the muddy grass. The dogs started barking and I leaned against the house, spitting out a big glob of mud. I waited for the dogs to quiet down.

I rested for a while, listening to the gentle coo of a faraway dove, then I tapped on Finch's windowsill. I waited, then tapped again. Finally he pushed up the shades and peered out. He didn't have his glasses on.

"It's just me," I whispered. "Help me up!" He reached out, grabbed me, and pulled me up through the window. I tumbled unceremoniously into his room. By the time I'd sat up, he'd pulled the shades back down.

"What are you doing here?" he whispered sleepily. He was wearing an old T-shirt with Daffy Duck saying "That's all Folks!" across the front. It was at least five years too small with a hole above the *k*, and what must've been Granger's plaid boxers because they went down to his knees. He looked embarrassed, then got back in bed and pulled the covers up to his chin.

I crawled on top of the bed.

"Isn't it Porky Pig who says, "That's all Folks?" I asked. "Where'd you get that old thing, anyway?" As soon as I said it, I felt bad, knowing that his mama had probably gotten it at the church thrift sale. But I was mad and hurt.

He just blinked at me. Finally I said, "I can't believe you betrayed me."

"I sent the drawing to the paleontologist," he said hesitantly, like he knew what was coming.

"He's at our house right now. He came. Can you believe that? He came all the way from Dallas. And you did it. I can't believe it. You did it. Was it because I didn't tell you about Granger?" I asked, tears in my eyes.

"No! Of course not!" he whispered. "You said you wanted to keep her a secret. You said you weren't ready and I was beginning to think you were right. But everyone's been saying that you all might lose the farm."

I stretched out on my back and looked at the ceiling. "I never thought in a million years when I gave you the drawing you'd betray me."

"The newspaper article was right inside the dinosaur book," he said. "All I had to do was ask Miss Ferriday to look the address up. You knew he'd come, didn't you? Somehow, some way."

"No," I said, tears rolling down my face. "I didn't. I never, ever thought you could do something like that to me."

"I did it for your family, Esme," he said. "And if you lost the farm, I'd lose you."

He'd done it for my family and for me. I looked over at him and saw his eyes tearing up. I turned away from Finch and we were quiet a good long time. I could hear the soft coo of the doves right outside his window now.

"Well, what did he say?" Finch said after a while. "Did you take him up the hill?"

"Yeah," I said. "He went up. And he says he's never seen anything like her. That she's worth a lot of money."

"Then why are *you* crying?"

"I don't know."

"Miss Lilah's dying," Finch said wearily as he reached over and wiped my face.

I touched my cheek where his fingers had just wiped away my tears, feeling the warmth. "I know."

When I woke up sometime later, Finch was sound asleep. He looked just like he did when he was little, in that holey Daffy Duck shirt, but I knew his world wasn't so simple anymore. I crept off the bed and went to the window. One of the dogs was sitting right outside, his eyes piercing, waiting.

I'd have to go out the front door. I tiptoed through the house and let myself out. I was carefully creeping down the porch steps when I realized someone was there in the semidarkness.

It was Pearl Mae, sitting on the swing, swaying back and forth and pushing off with her bare feet, her face like stone. I went on down the steps, but something made me turn back.

"Tell me where my Granger is," she said.

My toes started to hum and I closed my eyes a moment. "I don't know where. But he's nearby, Mrs. Aberdeen. He was away . . . and now he's come back."

She stopped swinging abruptly, and as I ran into

the night, I felt a tiny, every so tiny, ray of hope radiating through me. Perhaps there was some good that came with the gift of finding things.

When I reached our orchard, I thought I saw a figure swirling around in the peach trees. *June Rain*. I crept a little closer then stopped. Not June Rain, but a fine mist spinning around and around, round and round, gracefully like a dancer doing a pirouette. Then it disappeared, rising into the dark sky. *Lilah*. I stood there, staring at the darkness, not believing what I'd just seen.

Old Jack barked when I came through the kitchen door. He sniffed at my hands, then went back to the door, wriggling and whining to be let out.

"He thinks someone's out there," said Bee. She was sitting at the table drinking a cup of coffee.

"There is," I mumbled. "There *was*," I corrected myself. "But not anymore. I think perhaps Miss Lilah might have passed away."

"She did. A few hours ago. Miss Opal called. She went peacefully. It was her time."

"Yes, I know that," I said flatly. I sat across from

Bee, slumping down with a sigh.

"I was worried about you," Bee said.

I didn't believe her. She'd never worried about me, not for a minute.

"Where were you?" she asked.

"You don't know where?" I asked her sarcastically. "You can't see everything?"

She calmly took another sip of her coffee. I knew the answer to that now. That we couldn't see or feel everything, only a little. And sometimes the things we wanted to know the most, God kept from us.

"I think Granger might be back," I said. Old Jack sniffed at my feet, then licked my fingers. I rubbed his head.

"He had to come home someday." She took another long sip of coffee.

"Did you put the professor in Paps's room?" I asked.

"Nowhere else to put him. Flobelle locks her boardinghouse at eight o'clock sharp. He can stay there from now on."

"What is it you see when you find things?" I asked.

She looked out the window. "It's really not just *seeing* things, Esme, as you're probably discovering. It's everything. What I hear. How I taste. How I smell. All my senses working together, fine-tuned like a piano. You're just at the beginning, that's all. And you'll be different than me. Much different."

"But why us?"

"Everyone has intuition. We Hennessey girls just got a double dose of it. But there's an art to finding lost things, Esme. Give it time, be patient. Fine-tune it." She got up wearily and lingered in the kitchen doorway.

"I don't think I want it."

"Neither did I, Esme," said Bee. "Neither did I. I've asked the good Lord to take it back on more than one occasion, believe me. Eventually you'll have to come to peace with the fact that it is here to stay. Forever, Esme. Forever."

"What was it, Bee?" I asked her. "What happened to Harlan when he was a baby?"

"Oh, Esme, leave it," she said. "Let's go to sleep before the sun comes up."

CHAPTER 16

The house was eerily quiet when I woke up a few hours later. I looked out the window and saw that the professor's car was still parked in the drive. I threw on my T-shirt, my muddied overalls, and moccasins, scrambled downstairs, banged through the screen door, and ran up the hill as fast as my feet would take me. Sure enough, he was there on his knees and holding the tiniest little tool, no bigger than a toothpick, scraping away at Louella Goodbones's eye socket.

"So, what were you using to uncover it?" he asked.

I held my hands on my hips, trying not to breathe hard, not wanting him to know how mad I was. "One of my grandpa's tools," I finally told him, in between breaths. "A woodworking file, I think."

"Just as I thought," he murmured. "We're lucky you didn't do any substantial damage." Then he added, "But I can tell you were gentle with her."

"Gee, thanks," I said sarcastically. He continued to scrape away.

"I understand," he said. "You're not happy I'm here. You liked having a secret. You feel like she's all yours. And she always will be in a way, Esme McCauley. She's yours. *You* found her. That will never, ever change."

He leaned back, took his hat off, peering up at me. "You love her, don't you?"

I looked under the tractor to see if Bump was there, pretending I hadn't heard him.

"I'll love her, too, Esme. I promise."

I watched him work, watched him scrape at the dirt. I realized how I could have damaged her with my lack of expertise, and a lump grew in my throat.

"We don't know much about their eyesight," he started, knowing I was listening, "but we can tell something by the size and shape of the orbital cavity. The eye sockets are pointed forward for bifocal vision, making their visual acuity as sharp as a razor. She probably could see a fly on a boulder up to two miles away. Up here were the ears." He pointed at her skull. "Dinosaurs could hear a bird call from a mile away, did you know that? And the teeth. This one could probably bite a car in half if it wanted to. She needed those teeth. It was a hard, hard world to survive in."

"What did she eat?" I found myself saying, and then felt like I'd betrayed her by asking a question.

"Small rodents, other small dinosaurs—whatever it could catch. And if it had to, it ate plants, berries. We no longer think it was one or the other, but whatever it took to survive. Look here—" He pointed to one of her teeth. "There's wear on these teeth, here. They did most of the chomping. The ones in the back were for grinding, bone crushers. And here," he said. "Come feel." I leaned down to where he pointed to the top of her orbital cavity. I ran my finger across a rim of gentle bumps. "That could be a blinder, hooding its eyes from the sun. Or it could have been a low ridge of horns."

My eyes grew big as I stood back and looked at

her. I thought I knew a lot about what I'd uncovered. I didn't, not really. Professor Abramanov already knew more, knew so much more than me. More than I ever would.

"So tell me, Esme," he said. "Why do you think it's a female?"

I shrugged. "I don't know. I just do," I said. "Do you think it could be a her?"

"Not sure yet. It's a shot in the dark, Esme; unless we find her sitting on a nest of eggs we may never know. We have much to learn. There are many theories that females had extra 'finery' you might say—a ridgy back, or a crested brilled skull to attract the males. But some say it could be the other way around."

Out of the corner of my eye, I saw someone walking up the hill.

It was a man wearing ugly plaid pants and a hat. Around his neck was a fancy camera with a flash as big and shiny as a hubcap. I recognized him now. Gordy Haines. He'd been let go at his newspaper job in Paradise for making up quotes in news stories and had shown up at the *Hollis Register*.

"Professor T.?" I whispered. "Did you make a phone call this morning from our house?"

The professor glanced over at Gordy Haines, then kept on scraping. "Only to my department head. I wanted to get the ball rolling. He wouldn't have told anyone about this, though, I promise."

"We have a party line, Professor. You didn't know it, but you practically told the whole town." The professor stood up, brushing off his khakis, just in time to shake hands with the reporter.

"Lordy, Lordy. Well, what do we have here?" Gordy asked, although it was obvious he already knew. "I heard we had a T. rex, Professor Abramanov." He'd done his homework. "I guess that's just perfect for you since you're nicknamed T. Rex, isn't it?" Gordy didn't have much of a chin, and it disappeared completely under his goofy smile.

The professor grimaced. "No, not a T. rex, but something big nonetheless. Something really big. Esme McCauley here found it and has been excavating it. She sent me a drawing of it, and I was intrigued, and came to get a look at the bones myself."

Although Gordy was holding a pen and pad, he wasn't writing any of this down. His eyes were glued on Louella Goodbones.

"Well, if you don't mind, Professor, I'd like to take a photo of you and Esme for the *Register*. This is big news in Hollis. Bigger than anything we've had in a long time. This is something the whole world will be interested in." Gordy winked at me.

"No," I whispered.

Professor T. turned, shielding me from Gordy. "We don't have much choice now, Esme," he said in a low voice. "He'd probably come up here on the sly anyway and take his photos. I don't like it either, but the more publicity we get, the more she's going to be worth. And if everyone *was* listening like you said, they're all going to be here soon, snooping around, taking their own photos." He looked sincere, but I think he liked this course of events; somehow he'd come out on top.

Gordy had started snapping a few photos of Louella Goodbones while we talked. "Stop it! Stop it!" I yelled. "You don't have permission! You have no right, neither of you, to be up here!" I turned away, breathing hard, tears springing to my eyes.

Professor T. looked at Gordy and held up his hand. "She's right. Please. Stop. Give her a moment."

Gordy nodded but fired off another half dozen shots. Professor T. tilted his head at me, and I knew I had no choice. I was trapped.

I'm sorry, Louella Goodbones.

Finch was right. I knew it the minute I'd started that drawing, the minute I found that article on the professor. This was all my doing and I suddenly felt like I was going to throw up.

The flash went off again—everything blended together faster and faster, everything that had changed this summer, faster and faster, until the world went dark and the next thing I knew I was falling.

I could see several pairs of shoes surrounding me when I came to. Then I heard Bee yelling at Gordy Haines to get off her property, then Old Jack was licking my ear, then Bo's worried face loomed over me, inspecting me real close, nose to nose, then he disappeared from view. I peered around, my whole body tingling, taking a while to wake up. We weren't on Solace Hill anymore. I was in the shade, looking up at ripe peaches, and in the distance I could hear Miss Lilah's geese squawking. They'd made it through the fence again.

I glanced around. The professor. Did he carry me to the orchard? I focused on the layers of grime and dust and mud on his boots.

He held out his hand and helped me up. I looked down, embarrassed at the dirty clothes I'd thrown on that morning. I hadn't even brushed my hair or teeth and now I was going to be in the *Hollis Register* for the whole world to see. Bee was walking Gordy to his car, talking to him animatedly, Bo following behind. Old Jack was chasing the geese through the trees now as Sugar Pie watched disinterestedly from her pasture.

"I'm getting back to work," Professor T. said to me. "You coming?"

I shook my head, then ran off into the woods.

Bee told me that when Harlan was ten, he'd come home one time with six bee stings on his face. He resembled a giant red balloon with two little beady eyes. He'd said that he'd been hungry and decided to stick his hand straight into the hive and help himself to the honey. Bee told him he was a first-rate fool to do such a thing, that sometimes something that you love the most can hurt you. I'd feared those bees my whole life, but that's where I went now. I stayed a safe distance from the hives and watched the bees buzzing to and fro. Harlan had painted those hives years after he'd been stung, all those swirls, with not a care in the world that he'd be stung again.

I walked over and stuck my hand right in, deep down into the warm honey. I kept it there as the bees droned like tiny, busy, lawn mowers and waited for them to sting me. But nothing happened, nothing at all. I pulled my hand out a minute later, stepping back, looking at the hives in awe. I didn't want the honey anymore. I let the big, gooey glob drip slowly from my hand, watching the bees go on with their day as though I'd never even been there. Then my toes started to vibrate, and I knew something was up somewhere.

I headed toward Harlan's cabin, but then I heard

squealing and Jewell's little bell tinkling. I came upon her, sitting in the woods. She must have gotten out of her enclosure. Maybe that's what my toes had been feeling. I picked her up, but she squealed so I put her down. I ran on through the woods, Jewell trotting behind me until I reached Harlan's cabin. I left Jewell snuffling around in the bushes outside. I opened the door and walked straight into Granger Aberdeen. We both let out a scream and Granger fell back on his rear, knocking over one of Harlan's paintings.

"What are you doing here?" he yelled. He looked awful, like a rat straight from the sewer. He even had a little beard and he stunk to high heaven.

"This is my Daddy Harlan's place," I blurted out. "What are you doing here?" I looked around for any sign of Luther Stump or Johnny Wallet.

He laughed as he got up. "You don't think I know that, Weasie?"

I cringed. It suddenly struck me as really strange being here with him, and him calling me by that silly name from long ago, when he was wanted by the police.

"Did you do it, Granger?" I asked.

"Is that what everyone thinks?" He looked at me, his eyes wide. "Is that what my family thinks?"

I shrugged. "Your daddy searched for you high and low for a long time."

He seemed surprised by that, then sat down wearily on the one chair in the cabin as though he were a hundred years old. "It was Luther who shot that man. It was an accident. It was dark; we couldn't see. We'd been drinking. And then he was right there next to us, scaring the jeepers out of us. Looked like Rumpelstiltskin with that raggedy beard—talking funny, real strange. Said he was a traveling prophet. Said he was looking for someone."

The hairs on my arm rose. I leaned back on the door, wondering why he was telling it all to me.

"And then he asked for some of our whiskey, said a little sin wouldn't hurt anyone," Granger continued. "Luther was reaching over to pour him a cup when the gun went off. He died instantly. I would've helped him if I could, but there was nothing we could do. I've never been more scared in my life. We scattered, found each other, then traveled together for a while—"

"Where are the others?" I asked.

He shook his head. "I don't know. I left them in New Mexico. Hitched my way back here."

"Why did you come back, Granger?"

"I don't know. I'm tired and I'm hungry. Never been more hungry in my life."

"Why don't you come home with me," I said. "Bee will make you something. Everything will be okay."

He laughed at that, then shook his head. I opened the door and walked down the steps, thinking about Finch, thinking about what I was about to do. I picked up Jewell and held her close. She smelled of mint and herbs. Then finally Granger came out and followed us home.

When we walked through the kitchen door, Bee was baking her famous peach pies to take them to the Ames house where people were gathering for Miss Lilah's funeral. June Rain took Jewell from me and quickly left the kitchen. Bee didn't hardly say a word to Granger, but she fixed him a heaping plate of leftovers, then got him a piece of pie. When he was finished, she picked up the phone and called Sheriff Finney.

Later that afternoon, after the sheriff had taken Granger away, I thought about going to see Finch to explain what I'd done, but I didn't have the courage to do it. Finally I went up Solace Hill. The professor nodded to me and handed me something that looked like a tiny toothbrush, then showed me what to do. We worked side by side, me brushing the dust away from her backbone while he carefully worked on her teeth.

He didn't say a thing when I occasionally wiped away tears. Perhaps he thought I was wiping away sweat, but whatever he thought he didn't say a word. With each bit of dirt we removed, I knew I was one step closer to the day when Louella Goodbones would leave us.

"How long?" I asked, after an hour or so had passed.

"Several months," he answered. "Maybe longer. Sometimes it takes years. The earth is soft here, from all the rain. I'll be bringing more help in, of course."

"Your assistants?"

"Yes, and students, too, a few who are working on getting their degrees." He took a long gulp from a water canister.

It occurred to me that his nickname, T. Rex, really didn't fit him at all. Not really. I watched him work like an artist on Louella Goodbones. Although he was a big man, there was something gentle about him.

"What does it take, Professor T.?"

He paused a moment, running his hand through his hair. "To do what, Esme?"

"To become like you," I said, embarrassed for some reason. Ridiculous. Someone like me hoping to go to a university, learn big words. *And go away.*

"A paleontologist?" he said, smiling a little. "Is that something that you'd like to be, Esme McCauley?"

I shrugged. He went back to his scraping and then said, "Four years of undergraduate work; mine was in geology. Then a master's, later, if you want, a doctorate. It takes many years, patience, and work. But more than anything, it's about honoring the things that came before us, a love for the earth beneath your feet. It's as simple as that, Esme." He glanced over at me from under his hat as I ran my hand across Louella Goodbones's snout. *Loving the earth and what came before us.*

"Why hasn't your grandmother been up here?" the professor asked after a while. "To look around."

"She won't come up here, ever. My grandfather—Paps—died here. Several months ago." But I knew it was more than that, lots more that she wouldn't tell me.

Later that day I biked to Finch's house but no one was home. I rode on into Hollis to the Just Teasin'. I leaned my bike against the window and went in. There were three ladies under the hair dryers, but they all popped them up like jack-in-the-boxes when I came in. June Rain was setting a perm, while Jewell slept nearby in her carrier.

June Rain looked calm and peaceful. I kept thinking about what Granger had said about that man, that he'd come looking for someone he knew. Could it have been her Uncle Hen? Something down deep told me not to tell her, that her past was connected to all her bad spells. It wasn't just us, it was all that came before; even if a bird had once made a nest in his beard, it wasn't a happy story or she wouldn't be here hiding from it all.

"You did the right thing, honey," Sweetmaw whispered, handing me a bottle of Dr Pepper. Apparently the sheriff had already called her. "Sheriff Trueitt said since Granger's a minor and came home of his own accord, he won't be in big trouble." She whispered even lower. "Spoon's off on a bender, but his mama, she's already at the station. Sheriff True-itt's letting her visit with him a short while till he finishes questioning him."

Oh, God. *Finch. I'm sorry.* I turned away, briefly catching June Rain's eye. She smiled with that dreamy nothing's-going-on-in-my-head look, and I slunk down in one of the salon chairs, wishing I could disappear.

"I hear you found some bones up on Solace Hill," Lottie Broadway said as June Rain put a roller in her hair.

I didn't think I could open my mouth right now even if there was chocolate nut angel pie in front of me.

"Bones?" Miss Vera joined in from under her dryer. "Bones?"

Lottie leaned over and screamed in her ear, "Dinosaur bones! They found some dinosaur bones!"

And suddenly Finch was there outside the window, panting, his eyes wild. He looked like he'd run all the way from home. I stepped outside and walked down the sidewalk away from prying eyes.

"I just heard," he said, and I had to look away. "You found Granger and brought him home."

"Finch," I began. "I . . . I . . . ." But then he pulled me to him and hugged me, like he was never going to let go and I hugged him back, as though my life depended on it, too, that if I let go we'd be swallowed into the earth, right here on the sidewalk in downtown Hollis. And I knew then I'd done the right thing and that tiny ray of hope that was curled up inside of me unfurled a tiny bit more.

CHAPTER 17

All heck broke loose the next morning. The *Hollis Register* put the photo of Professor T. and me right on the front page—I looked like I'd just rolled out of bed, my big ears sticking out through my messy cocoon hair, and there was an ink mark across my lip, like I had a moustache. The story of Granger being detained was tiny, buried in the paper, with no mention, thank God, that it was me who'd found him. Bee brought the paper in just as the phone started ringing, and it didn't stop for hours. The news had spread across the wires, whatever those were, and people interested in the dinosaur bones, reporters, collectors, museums, all of them were calling Bee. She was cussing herself out that she'd shaken hands on a deal with the professor.

We were supposed to be getting ready for Miss Lilah's funeral at the Holy Mercy Church of Abiding Faith. But as we scurried around, cars started pulling up to the house, lookey-loos wanting to get a gander at Louella Goodbones. It hurt more than anything in the world to think of all these people traipsing up my hill, walking all over her, and Paps. Old Jack galloped around the house barking up a storm as we all ran outside. Luckily the professor turned them away, explaining the damage they could do, and Bee put a makeshift "No Trespassing" sign up at the front of the drive. The professor went back to work and we drove off in the Bee Wagon, the smell of peach pies wafting up from the way back.

June Rain came with us. She hadn't stepped foot in a church forever, but she came all right. Bee'd put her foot down and said pigs, even if they were gussied up, were not allowed in church, so Jewell was home in her enclosure. June Rain had on her best dress, that one with embroidered roses that Harlan had bought her in Mexico, and her hair was all shiny. She'd put on a little of her Charisma perfume that Harlan had given her for Christmas three years ago. I glanced back at her and smiled and she smiled back.

I turned back around wondering why she was doing better. I was worried that the suitcase under her bed was packed. My feet started to vibrate, but they quieted down as we pulled into the church parking lot. Sweetmaw arrived just as we did and walked in with us.

Everyone was looking at us slyly during the sermon. We sat next to Miss Opal in the front row, because she had no one else, no family to tend to her. Reverend Hopper talked about Miss Lilah's long life and good heart, and Bee snorted, then pretended to wipe her nose.

I kept looking for Finch, hoping he'd come and finally he did, slipping into the pew next to me. Bo colored on the church bulletin with the orange crayon Bee let him bring in his pocket. I glanced down and saw that his picture was a bunch of swirls and blobs and looked a lot like Harlan's work, only better, and I realized then how childlike Harlan's paintings were, so quickly done, but with a purpose, and that was a good thing in its own way.

I glanced back and saw Dove and Rose and Mady sitting in the back. Dove and Rose smiled at me, and I knew it was for more than just being famous in the newspaper.

Something was really bothering Bee. She kept shifting around in her seat and scratching at her arms. Maybe it was the deal she'd made with the professor. Maybe she was thinking we could've gotten more money. But I was at peace with it. He'd take care of Louella, and I knew it had to be enough to save the farm. Bee used to say not to ever ask God for more than He gives you. It was enough, and that was all that mattered. But then something deep down inside began to gnaw at me, too. An inkling. A slow buzz in the pit of my stomach. Then in my toes, which I started tapping on the floor trying to make it go away. I didn't need to find anything more, not ever again. I started wiggling around in my seat, too, till Bee pinched me.

As we started to file out of the church one by one, everyone greeting us and remarking on the dinosaur bones, and others patting Finch's head and telling him everything was going to be all right, my feet started to vibrate in earnest. By the time we got in the Bee Wagon and were heading down the road, they were on fire.

Bee was still acting funny. She drove right past the Ames property, her foot on the gas, not even looking at all the other cars pulling in for the after-the-funeral gathering.

"Sweetmaw will be wondering where . . ." June Rain trailed off.

There was complete silence in the car as we turned down our drive, past our new "No Trespassing" sign. Bee took her foot off the gas then, going real slow now, looking to the right then the left. Then she rolled down her window and I saw her nostrils flare, like Old Jack when he picks up a scent.

Sugar Pie was free again, and Old Jack was barking somewhere, and Jewell's little face peered at us from her enclosure. Nothing seemed out of the ordinary. But the hair on my neck stood straight up.

June Rain saw it first. She was out of the Wagon before Bee had even pulled it to a complete stop. Bee cussed as she slammed the brakes. Then Bo squealed like a mouse and he jumped out of the car, too. Finch put his hand on my leg as though to brace me for what was to come. I could see something big and white at the top of Solace Hill billowing in the wind and I realized what it was; the professor had set up a work tent over Louella Goodbones. Then Finch turned my chin toward what was right in front of us. Harlan's truck.

CHAPTER 18

I leaned against the Bee Wagon as my family scurried up the steps and through the screen door.

I stared at the tent on Solace Hill. The professor was up there digging away, oblivious to the goings-on down at the house, or perhaps not. Finch got out of the car a moment later and stood next to me.

"Go on," he said to me. "You can't stay here forever."

"Will you come with me?"

"Sorry." Finch shook his head. "I want to pay my respects to Miss Opal. Then see Granger. Mama's bringing him home today." He trailed off and looked away.

"That's okay," I said.

He gave me a hug, then turned and walked down the drive.

I looked at Harlan's truck, thinking about all the times I'd watched for it, listened for it, waited for it. Hundreds of times. How all of us, even Bee, had waited for him. And now he was finally here. My daddy was home and I wasn't sure if I really cared anymore.

Harlan was leaning nonchalantly against one of the counters. Bo was clinging to his legs and June Rain was clutching tight, too, like she was never going to let him go. They looked like desperate bugs. Even Old Jack, the traitor, was there lying like a frog-dog, his feet splayed out in back, his tail thumping on the floor. Bee was washing dishes, her back firmly to them, and I wondered if she'd even looked at him yet. The phone was ringing, but Bee ignored it. We all did.

"I suppose you heard the news about Esme's dinosaur," said Bee finally, her back still to us. "That's why you're home, isn't it, Harlan?"

I looked at Harlan. He hadn't noticed me yet, 'cause he was looking into June Rain's eyes just the way I imagined he'd done the first time he saw her under the revival tent over in Paradise. I stood staring at him, my handsome daddy who I hadn't seen in three years. His jet-black hair was long and there were crow's feet around his eyes. He was wearing a denim shirt, and there were bright splatters of paint down the leg of his jeans. My eyes traveled down to his feet. He had on what looked like a brand-new pair of shiny black boots. No rainbow boots.

Bo seemed to notice at the same time. He kneeled down, studying those new boots, probably looking for his rainbows, but of course they weren't there. Those boots were on a bearded man named Wilson Henry, lying in the morgue in Paradise. Did Harlan know that?

"Where's my rainbows?" Bo said, and Harlan looked down, quickly hiding a small frown. Bee's shoulders tensed up at the sink; she was waiting for Harlan's answer, too.

"Lost them in a bet." Harlan laughed. "You'll have to paint on some more, my sweet Bobo."

Bee went on washing the dishes, clanking them together as the phone rang. *Ring, ring, ring ring ring. Ring, ring, ring ring ring.*

"You didn't answer me," Bee said. "Did you hear the news?" *Ring, ring, ring ring ring.* Bee grabbed the phone and took it off the hook, then went back to the dishes, all without looking at Harlan.

Harlan smiled. "Of course, heard on the radio. But I was already on my way home anyway. Just outside of San Antonio." He suddenly noticed me standing there.

"Whoa!" he exclaimed. "It's Esme. You got big!"

Harlan reached for me, but I slipped from his grasp, just in time. As I left the room, I heard him mutter casually as though he didn't have a care in the world, "She's always the hard one, that Esme."

"She misses you the most, don't you know that?" said Bee. But I'd already run outside, letting the screen door slam, wishing more than anything I could scream at the top of my lungs forever and forever. I didn't hear his reply.

I put Sugar Pie back in her pasture, fighting tears as I leaned into her. I wasn't gonna cry over Harlan McCauley. No sirree. Never. The Bee Wagon came down the drive a few minutes later and Bee pulled over, rolling down the window. Several peach pies were on the floorboard and a covered casserole was next to her on the passenger seat.

"I'm going over to Miss Lilah's for a little bit. Pay our respects. Want to come?"

I turned from her so she couldn't see me wipe my eyes. "Nope," I said. Miss Lilah had come to say good-bye to me already. She'd understand why I didn't want to go now.

"Suit yourself."

"Will it be enough, the money?" I asked. "Enough to save the farm?"

Her eyes softened. "Yes, Esme, it's more than enough. You found her for us, didn't you?"

"No," I said. "Paps did."

The corner of her mouth twitched, transforming that unsmile into an almost, perhaps, sort-of smile, and the tears sprung to my eyes again, but these were happy tears. She hit the gas and pulled on down the drive, the curtains in the back swaying to and fro. I watched her go until a cloud of dust finally obscured the Wagon.

Is he going to stay this time, Bee? Is my daddy

going to stay? Oh, how I wanted to scream it after her.

I went up the hill and under the big white work tent. The professor looked up briefly, then got back to work. I watched him scraping and brushing patiently, quietly, over and over in the same area. I leaned against one of the tent poles and ran my hand over canvas. Finally I said, "My daddy came home." I waited to see his reaction, but there wasn't one. He just kept on scraping, the soft sounds soothing, like the rhythm of Bee's sewing machine, only he was releasing Louella Goodbones from the earth. He loved her already, I could see that now.

"Do you want to help, Esme?" he asked.

"Okay," I answered.

He handed me a tiny brush and we worked side by side.

Later, walking back to the house, I found a little box sitting on the back steps. I opened it up. It was a telephone-wire ring, just like the other girls', twisted up wildly into a blooming flower, a teeny tiny dinosaur peeking up from the center.

* * *

We had a leftover casserole for dinner. Opal had sent it home with Bee. Bee plopped a can of mushroom soup and sprinkled Frosted Flakes on top to make it look fresh. Sweetmaw swatted Harlan when she saw him, then gave him a big kiss. Everyone sat around the table hardly talking, just the *crunch, crunch* of the Frosted Flakes while the professor and Harlan stared at each other. June Rain held Jewell close and barely looked up from her food. The professor said he'd be leaving soon and coming back with his students in a few days.

I snuck out of the house after everyone had gone to bed. It was a clear night; the stars shone through the limbs of the trees, radiating like pinwheels. I saw a tiny glimmer of red hovering in the darkness. It was Harlan, leaning against a tree, smoking. A shiver went up my spine. Had it been Harlan all along?

"You know you can't hate me forever." What a strange figure he made, my daddy leaning against that tree like a specter who'd been thrown up from the darkness.

I laughed. "Oh, yes I can."

He took another long drag of his cigarette. "Well, I guess you can, Esme," he said.

"Are you leaving soon?" I yelled. "That's all I want to know! When are you leaving?"

He stood there, not saying a word. "Is that what you want?" he asked after a while. "Do you want me to leave?"

"You know if you leave again, she won't forgive you. Not this time. Every time you go, she disappears a little more. There's not much left. You can't see it, 'cause you don't see anything. You will lose her if you leave again."

"Wow," he said. "When did my little baby girl grow up?"

"While you were gone," I said. "And I was never your little baby."

"No, you weren't." He laughed. "You were always grown-up even if you came so early, and I'm sorry if somehow I made you that way."

"Wow. That's profound. I didn't think you were ever sorry for anything you've ever done in your life."

He looked away. "I'm a wanderer, Esme, that's all it is."

"That's not a good enough answer and you know it."

Somewhere in the distance Sugar Pie neighed, as though telling me to stop.

"Maybe I'll work on stayer longer this time," he said.

"Well, you just go on and do that, while you're here for all of one minute," I said sarcastically, knowing that he'd never do it, 'cause he never followed through on any of his promises, none of them, big or small.

"I envy him." For just a millisecond I thought he meant the professor, "Bobo," he added. "Envy his carefree view of life. And you, Esme, you take it too deeply, always have."

"I'm only twelve years old, Harlan," I said. *I'm still a child and I need you.*

He turned to leave.

"Why leave us? What do you do while you're gone?"

"I travel, see the world. I paint," he said. "And I breathe. It's as simple as that."

"So you can't breathe when you're with us?" And I thought to myself, it was true, he'd always been holding his breath when he was with us, while June Rain seemed to be slowly letting hers out.

"It's not *you*; it's not any of you. This is about me," he said in the darkness.

It's always been just about you. It always has. And none of us.

"So just how did you lose your rainbow boots? Bo's really sad about that, if you hadn't noticed."

He narrowed his eyes at me. "Someone I was traveling with for a few months, a man named Wilson Henry, bet me twenty bucks I couldn't name the fifty-one states. I lost the bet and he got the boots. We parted ways not long after that. Said he was going to go find his kin."

"There's fifty states," I mumbled, feeling sick that Harlan might have led this man to us, to his death, even if he didn't know it.

"I guess that's why I lost."

"And did he ever see your paintings, this man?"

"Why, sure he did," Harlan said, taking a puff. "He said my June Rain was the most beautiful girl he'd ever seen and I was the luckiest man in the world. Said I should go home to her. And I thought perhaps I would. Why all these questions, Esme? Does it really matter what I do when I'm gone?

Can't you forgive your daddy?"

He was still waiting for my answer, staring at me, but I couldn't say it out loud. The words burned on my lips. *Because you didn't come home right away when you knew Paps had died, when you knew we'd all be hurting, and needed you. You still didn't come home, not until you found out about the dinosaur bones.* And some fragile cord, tiny and tender, that had connected us, father and daughter, snapped, and I thought perhaps I might die at that very second. He dropped his cigarette and stepped on it before walking away. I stifled a sob.

I realized then I wasn't alone. The professor was there behind me, leaning against his car. He'd been watching, too. "You okay, Esme?" he asked quietly, his face hidden under his hat.

"Uh-huh," I answered, swiping a tear. Thank goodness it was dark.

"I'm leaving in the morning. I'll be back in a few days," he said as he opened his car door. "We'll continue. Lots of work ahead of us. Lots to learn." He paused a moment as though he was going to say more, but then got in his car and drove on down the drive.

CHAPTER 19

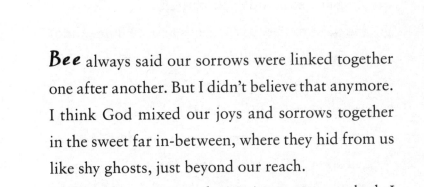

Bee always said our sorrows were linked together one after another. But I didn't believe that anymore. I think God mixed our joys and sorrows together in the sweet far in-between, where they hid from us like shy ghosts, just beyond our reach.

The next morning, laying in my cocoon bed, I thought about how the professor was leaving us for a few days. He said he would be back, and unlike Harlan, I believed him. He'd be back, and he'd take Louella Goodbones away eventually. But it was okay. She was meant to be taken away from here so we could all stay.

I looked out the window and saw Harlan carrying a paint box and a small canvas. He headed toward the woods, and I guessed he was on his way to his cabin.

I was turning away from the window when I realized I could hear the low hum of another car. I could feel it in my toes. It wasn't good, whatever it was, this car. It wasn't good. I leaned out the window for a better look and saw it was Mr. Galloway's shiny Cadillac.

Bee must've sensed it, too, 'cause, she flew into the yard just as he was getting out.

"I'm sure you heard the news about Esme's dinosaur," she said. "We'll have the money soon, Mr. Galloway. More than enough."

There was a strange pleading in her voice, like she knew another sorrow was coming down to us.

"I'm sorry, Mrs. McCauley," Mr. Galloway said, handing her a stack of papers. "Homer had mortgaged the farm, yes, but what I hadn't remembered until I went back through the papers yesterday is that someone had sold the deed to that hill many, many years ago."

Sold the hill. The words sunk down deep in me, like anchors, and I closed my eyes, reeling.

Bee took the papers but didn't read them. "What kind of damnation trick is this?" she hollered.

"It all came back to me yesterday. Over thirty

years ago you came in, Bee, said you needed fifty dollars in gold coins, wanted to sell 'that damn blasted hill,' I believe were your words."

They both glared at each other as the morning cicadas droned around them.

Sold the hill. Bee had sold the hill. I sank down to my knees, my head resting on the windowsill, barely listening.

"Well, spit it out then," Bee said wearily. The fight seemed to have gone out of her. "What is it you've come to say?"

"The bank owns the rights to the dinosaur, Bee," he said quietly, even a little sadly.

Bo joined me. He knelt down and rested his head on one of my knees, patting the other over and over as I strained to hear. I poked my head up again.

"We'll fight this," Bee finally said, her head bobbing, as though she were about to cry. "You're taking advantage of a little girl. Taking away her dreams, the one triumph of her life. You don't know what she's been through. What we've all been through. Everyone will stand behind her. Your bank will be vilified."

Mr. Galloway cleared his throat. "Everyone knows what you've been through," he said. "But you don't have the money to fight the bank, Bee, plain and simple."

She thrust those papers at him, but he wouldn't take them. He backed away, back into his shiny car, and drove off.

Finally Bee's fingers uncurled and the papers scattered around her.

I grabbed his plastic soldiers, which he'd left in my bed, and told Bo to go play in his room. I tiptoed past June Rain's room, then downstairs and out the back door. At the top of Solace Hill, I crawled under the tractor once more.

"Good-bye, Louella Goodbones," I said softly. *Good-bye.*

She really wasn't mine anymore, if she'd ever been. Bump hopped across my chest, then down to Louella Goodbones's crest. He hopped on over her and continued down the hill.

I found Bee sitting on the back steps, by the screen door, her face stricken. "What is it?" I asked. "Why was Paps on that hill that day with the tractor and what does it have to do with Harlan when he was a baby? And did you really sell Solace Hill? What's it all got to do with the other?"

She swallowed and looked down. "Sometimes, like I told you, something willows its way up whether you want it or not—a spirit, a ghost, whatever it is, it comes to show you something that you must know."

I sat down next to her and looked off into the distance toward Solace Hill.

"When Harlan was a baby," she continued, "a ghost would come every night, take him from his crib and walk him up Solace Hill, and then promptly at midnight bring him back down and put him back in his crib. Homer never knew, slept through it all with that loud-as-a-train snore." Shivers went up my arms. "I'd watch that ghost light go up and down, up and down every night, afraid my baby would die out there in the cold. But there was nothing to do. I was powerless."

"And what was Harlan's ghost trying to tell you, Bee?"

"That my child was not meant to be with us, that he was a wanderer, meant to wander the earth. I begged for anything, anything to make the ghost leave, to leave my baby alone. And the ghost told me that if I buried a box of gold coins, it would leave for good. So I sold the hill, put the coins in the box, and buried it. And the ghost left. For good. And Harlan's been leaving us just like the ghost said." She stifled a sob.

Harlan's been leaving us just like the ghost said.

"And then Paps found the bill of sale for the hill," she continued. "Took him about a week before he got the whole story out of me. He didn't believe the part about the ghost but believed me about the box of coins. That's what he was doing, Esme, trying to dig up the box to save the farm; those gold coins would be worth a fortune now. And maybe he thought by bringing it up, he'd bring Harlan home, too."

"But I found the box, Bee, and there was only one coin in it."

"When Homer drove up that hill, I didn't know it'd been cleaned out." She shook her head, confused. "Only thing I can think of is Harlan. I told him the story years back; I felt he needed to know he was born that way, a wanderer. And that he couldn't help it."

"Well, what'd he do with the money?" I asked after a moment.

"Probably paid off some gambling debt, who knows." She snorted.

Harlan. He could have helped to save the farm, way back before it had gotten so bad. Way before Paps drove his tractor up the hill.

Bee put her head in her hands and started to cry. And knowing that even Bee didn't know what to do made me feel a tenderness toward her that I thought I'd never feel in a gazillion years. I heard the soft tinkling of Jewell's bell behind us through the screen door and knew June Rain was listening.

Bo was playing outside with a stick, Old Jack chasing after him, later that afternoon. Harlan's truck was still in the drive. I figured he was off in the woods painting, oblivious to everything going on back here. Sweetmaw was in the kitchen sipping coffee with Bee, both silent, those papers laid out in front of them across the table. I thought of Professor T. and his patient hands showing me how to work on the bones. He was probably already on the road back to Dallas, but I could still feel him here with us, with Louella Goodbones. He'd be back; I knew he would.

"I'm real sorry, honey," Sweetmaw said to me as I plopped down at the table. "I made some calls; it appears the bank does own the hill."

I looked at the two of them, those sisters who'd been held apart for so many years. Now united over all our sorrows.

I caught eyes with June Rain as she drifted by with the coffeepot. She briefly laid the tips of her fingers on my shoulder, and a tender shiver went up my back.

We all seemed to notice the shadow in the screen door at the same time. Harlan stood there. June Rain set the coffeepot down and stood on the other side of the door. She lifted her hand for just a second, and he stood still as a statue, with a sadness that seemed to say *I can't help it, I can't help it.*

Later I went upstairs and found June Rain

sobbing in her bed. I crawled under the covers with her, rolled up to her, and laid my head on her shoulder as she continued to sob.

After a while she said, "You were so small. They told me you weren't going to make it. I couldn't risk losing you, too, that's all. Bee saved you, made sure you lived, but by then my heart had already broken."

Maybe I no longer needed to worry about the suitcase.

In the middle of the night, Bo had joined us, and at some point curled up under her arm like a doodlebug.

I whispered to June Rain, "Did you know him? Wilson Henry? Was he your Uncle Hen?"

For a long time she lay quiet. "That was his name, yes. I think it must have been him. Come to find me, somehow, some way. He wasn't a good man, Esme. And my family was not good either."

Bo started to stir. When I opened my mouth to ask another question, she put her finger on my lips to quiet me. Then later, in the early morning dawn,

I crept out of June Rain's bed. I pulled the covers up and over her and Bo and went downstairs. As I was tiptoeing down the back hallway, I saw Harlan standing in the doorway of Paps's room. I stood there watching him. I saw sadness perched there in his eyes. Bee says sometimes our regrets are squashed down so deep we don't know them anymore. Harlan walked past and handed me something, then went on down the hallway. A moment later, I heard the screen door slam. I waited a few seconds before looking down. It was the photo of June Rain in the prairie dress. I guess Bee had given it back to him, so he'd see his regrets. I went out the back door, got on my bicycle, and rode toward town.

And then a couple of weeks later, in the beginning of July, God proved me wrong and finally gave us a joy, a joy after all those honeycomb sorrows. I was sitting at the table eating a slice of meat loaf that Bee was making me eat because I hadn't been able to eat dinner. Bee'd been on the phone for a while, wrapping the cord around into the hallway so I couldn't hear.

After she hung up, Bee sat down across from me, shaking her head real slow in disbelief. "Seems the will's been read and Lilah left Miss Opal the land and the house and enough to live on the rest of her life."

"That's great," I said, but Bee held up her hand.

"There's more. She left Finch ten thousand dollars. With the provision that Finch uses it to go to college and his family can't touch it. She left you a thousand dollars. I guess she figured Finch was going to need it more."

I knew that was true.

"And is there a provision on my money?" I asked, stunned.

"No, no provision," Bee said. "You can do what you want."

"Is that enough for the farm?"

"It's enough to buy back Solace Hill after the dinosaur's all gone," Bee said. "If that's what you'd like." I opened my mouth to speak but she interrupted me. "There's more news. Violet Galloway's been furious with her husband, it seems. Says they have enough money. Hired a lawyer to look into it all. You have finding rights, Esme. You found it straight and square. It would have never been found without you." *And without Paps, and Bee's gift, and perhaps Harlan after all, or else Paps wouldn't have been up there in the first place digging.* "The bank is going to offer you a nice sum of money. A finding fee."

"And will that be enough?" I asked her. "For the rest of the farm?"

She nodded her head and a warm shiver of relief spread through me. "But don't you want to go to college?" she said.

I thought about what I'd asked the professor, about getting all those degrees like him. Of digging in the earth someday, honoring it and loving it like he'd said.

"We'll solve that problem when we get there," I said. "Let's use it to save the farm, to save us."

CHAPTER 20

Bee always said life was about leavings and comings, but I think it's also about those who stay. Harlan painted up a storm of "ain't-no-picture" paintings the rest of that summer that were strangely absent of June Rain, then one day he left. I was picking the last of the peaches when he rolled his truck to a stop nearby. His arm rested on the open window, his fingers tapping to the beat of "Raindrops Keep Fallin' on My Head" blaring from the radio. It was all over between him and June Rain. But I knew that wasn't why he was leaving. He'd been leaving us forever, since that ghost took him up and down Solace Hill.

"Bye, Esme," he said, giving me a little salute like handsome men do in the movies when they're going off to war. "I'll be back soon. Don't grow up too much this time."

I wanted to ask him what he'd done with the buried coins, but it didn't matter now. He waited a moment more, perhaps for me to say something. Then flicked a cigarette butt out the window, and gunned the motor, and drove away. I watched till he was out of sight, not knowing if I felt anything at all about him anymore. I looked at the fading cigarette ember, then stepped on it, extinguishing it.

I put the peaches in a basket, then started for the house. Old Jack joined me in the early morning chill, whining and licking my hands. Then he ran off and I followed him till we reached the bottom of Solace Hill. This small bump of a mountain that had held so many secrets for millions of years, then finally released them to the world. It was so empty now.

The professor's crew had to remove Paps's tractor to take Louella Goodbones away. Bee said I could keep it, so we put it in front of the fence to block where Lilah's geese always get out, and so we could see it every time we pulled up the drive. Bee said we could decorate it with hay bales and pumpkins and at Christmastime drape a strand of twinkle lights on it.

The professor had come and gone all summer, even after school started in September, working with his crew, me quietly by his side, handing him tools. Bee invited everyone in for dinner at night, and I'd sit mesmerized as they told stories of digs in faraway places and mysterious fossils brought up. I peppered them all with a thousand questions as Bee went around the table topping off their sweet teas and plopping second helpings on their plates.

And then one day we watched the crew carefully load the very last bone onto a huge flatbed truck. Professor T. and I stood reverently at the bottom of Solace Hill watching. He held his safari hat at his chest.

I hadn't said a word all morning. I couldn't.

"I named her Esmesaurus," Professor T. said as we turned to watch the truck go down the drive. "They can never take that away from you. She will go down in history with your name."

And still, I couldn't speak; I was too busy absorbing my joy.

• • •

The *Register* covered the removal of the last dinosaur bone, complete with photos of the huge crane, and once again the news was picked up all across the county and the whole state, even as far away as the Museum of Natural History in New York City, and some places overseas, too. Invitations came from all over the place addressed to "Esme McCauley, Dinosaur Finder, and Professor T. Rex Abramanov" to speak about our amazing new dinosaur, along with some speaking fees, which the professor said were all mine to do with as I wished. Bee said she'd start an account over at the bank in Paradise for my college fund.

Later that year I made my first speech in Dallas, at SMU, when they officially announced their acquisition and an anonymous donation for the study and future display of Esmesaurus. My whole class attended, even Miss Ferriday and Mrs. Greenly from Paradise. Bee, Sweetmaw, June Rain, and Bo sat in the front row. I talked about Solace Hill, and that first night following the fireflies up and up till I tripped over the bone and how someday I wanted to be a paleontologist. Finch, Dovie, Rose, and Mady clapped the loudest when I'd finished. I'd sprouted a few inches by then and Bee says I was finally growing into my face and into my true self, just like she said I would.

Professor Abramanov came to see us every now and then, even after they took the bones away. He dug small holes up and around Solace Hill, "just in case," he'd say, meaning there might be more fossils below. But I think we both knew Louella Goodbones was best.

"Esmesaurus." I murmured her name, her *new* name, as Old Jack and I stood at the bottom of Solace Hill, my feet buzzing with the knowing that I was slowly learning to harness and to finetune, that knowing that I was about to find something. My gift that I no longer regretted opening. And there at the top of the hill was a figure. *Paps.* I shielded my eyes. Old Jack whined but stood still next to me. Paps waved to us, then disappeared on down the other side of Solace Hill. Good-bye, Paps. Good-bye, Louella Goodbones.

Finch was coming over for an early breakfast and

would be here soon. I could see the professor's car as it slowly came up the drive, surely, patiently, just like him. His eyes, as usual, shadowed under that weathered hat. He waved to me. I looked back over my shoulder, shielding my eyes as the sun moved up over Solace Hill. Then Old Jack and I turned and walked on home.